Alexander Fullerton was a submarine officer during the Second World War. Since leaving the Navy he has worked in shipping and in publishing, but for some years now has been a full-time writer. His impressive list of best-sellers includes *A Wren Called Smith*, *Surface!* and *Store*. He now lives in the Republic of Ireland.

Reviews of *The Thunder and the Flame:*

'An exciting retelling of this famous incident'
Daily Telegraph

'Excellent battle scenes reeking of blood and black powder'
Evening Standard

'Vivid, forceful and fast-moving'
Bristol Evening Post

Also by
Alexander Fullerton

SURFACE!
BURY THE PAST
NO MAN'S MISTRESS
A WREN CALLED SMITH
THE WHITE MEN SANG
THE YELLOW FORD
THE WAITING GAME
SOLDIER FROM THE SEA
LIONHEART
CHIEF EXECUTIVE
THE PUBLISHER
STORE
THE ESCAPISTS

Alexander Fullerton

The Thunder and the Flame

'In the year 1591 was that memorable
Fight of an English ship called the
Revenge, under the command of Sr Richard
Greenvill; Memorable (I say) even
beyond credit, and to the Height of
some Heroicall Fable.'

Sir Francis Bacon

MAYFLOWER
GRANADA PUBLISHING
London Toronto Sydney New York

Published by Granada Publishing Limited
in Mayflower Books 1978

ISBN 0 583 12530 1

First published in Great Britain by
Peter Davies Ltd 1964
Copyright © Alexander Fullerton 1964

Granada Publishing Limited
Frogmore, St Albans, Herts AL2 2NF
and
3 Upper James Street, London W1R 4BP
1221 Avenue of the Americas, New York, NY 10020, USA
117 York Street, Sydney, NSW 2000, Australia
100 Skyway Avenue, Toronto, Ontario, Canada M9W 3A6
Trio City, Coventry Street, Johannesburg 2001, South Africa
CML Centre, Queen & Wyndham, Auckland 1, New Zealand

Made and printed in Great Britain by Cox & Wyman Ltd,
London, Reading and Fakenham
Set in Intertype Times

Some Notes and Acknowledgements

This is a novel. But it is based on the results of careful research, and every fact which is on record, and which I have been able to find, has been taken into account and used in the story's framework. Where no facts are on record, I have bridged the gaps by using imagination, common sense and a basic knowledge of seamanship; and I believe now that this is a reasonably true picture of that battle which may still be regarded as the most dramatic naval engagement ever fought.

But it *is* a novel, and in order to make it (I hope) a rounded story, I have invented certain names and characters to play supporting roles. Philip Gawdy was there, all right, in 1591; so was Langhorne, *Revenge*'s captain. But nearly all the names of sailors had to be invented.

A bibliography has no place in a work of fiction. In case, however, a reader might wish to check or dispute the known facts of that fight in the Azores, I would say that my basic sources have been Ralegh, Linschoten, Monson, Hawkins, Gawdy's letters, and documents in the Naval Museum in Madrid.

Professor A. L. Rowse's splendid biography, *Sir Richard Grenville of the Revenge*, has been a most useful source of reference on Grenville's earlier career, and I am greatly indebted to him and his book for that; but I must record that my reconstruction of the battle differs basically from his own deductions. I mention this only for the information of critics who might not otherwise appreciate that the variations in my version are the results of serious analysis.

For assistance in the processes of research, I would like to thank Professor Christopher Lloyd of the Royal Naval College at Greenwich. My debt to him goes back more than twenty years, since it was he who, as my tutor at the Royal Naval College, Dartmouth, first infected me with an interest in naval history. Also at Greenwich, but in the National Maritime Museum, Lieutenant Commander George Naish, R.N.R., gave me very real help. Again from Greenwich, Professor Michael Lewis, whose articles (now a book) *Armada Guns* I had already found as useful as they are fascinating, was kind enough to provide the answer, and by telephone at that, to a technical question which until then had baffled me and was beginning to cause insomnia.

For technical advice, for reading the typescript, and for confirming and expanding my own theories on what happened in the early stages of the action off Flores, I am more than grateful to Captain Donald Macintyre, D.S.O., D.S.C., Royal Navy.

In Madrid, I was encouraged by the courteous assistance of Admiral Julio Guillen, Director of the Naval Museum; also in Madrid, the collaboration of Don Santiago Fernandez Jimenez was extremely valuable. I hope those gentlemen will forgive me if they find my story to be written from a nationalistic viewpoint.

I would like to acknowledge the efficient help which I received from the staffs of the Reading Room and North Library at the British Museum, and from the staff of the Round Room at the Public Records Office.

Finally, in fact belatedly, I must congratulate my wife on her quite extraordinary patience; and that brings me to a dedication, which is:

TO

JOHN, SIMON AND GILES

Prologue

England thirsted for Spanish Gold.

It came yearly in the treasure fleets, the *flotas* from the Indies, Spain's colonies in the New World; it came in convoys of great argosies that wallowed over the Atlantic under white bellies of canvas and the banners of Holy Spain.

Formerly the hulks had come singly and in groups or lesser squadrons; but so many had fallen to the English ships – to Queen's ships or to corsairs and 'ships of reprisal' – that in more recent years Philip had brought his treasure home in fleets of up to a hundred sail, massed together for mutual protection and defended by ships of war against the English pirates.

Spain lived and fought on the treasure from her empire; so to Elizabeth of England there was double value in its interception by her captains.

Two years ago – in 1589 – the Earl of Cumberland had been in the Azores with English ships to reap the immense rewards of a year of Spanish overlordship in her colonies; but the convoys – there were two – eluded him, and won past Frobisher as well, who was farther to the east. And at the turn of the year a royal edict had kept Sir John Hawkins in port when his ships were ready, manned and victualled and he would rather have been at sea – which was surely where a gentleman of the West Country belonged when Spanish loot was in the offing – and yet another treasure fleet swam safely into Iberian ports.

Wasted opportunities indeed: and these at a time when Spain could have no warships, or precious few, fit to defend her merchant shipping. Only the year before, in 1588, her great Armada had been shattered in the Channel and on the coasts of Ireland. It had been intelligence of a new muster of Spanish sails at Ferrol and Corunna, and talk of new galleons built and building – in particular, rumour of twelve great ones referred to as *The Twelve Apostles* – that had caused Elizabeth to hold back Hawkins in the fear of a new descent on England.

These fears were dispelled, as a nightmare ends at dawn; but it was a dawn that came too late. When the Lord Admiral ordered Hawkins and Frobisher away, each with a squadron of the Queen's ships, the Spaniards held their convoys in the Indies, waiting for the English to be back in English ports – which they were, before the year was out. English corsairs haunted the Spanish Indies all that winter while the Spaniards lay alongside wooden jetties or swung at moorings in well-sheltered anchorages, and the wealth that belonged to Philip came out of the mines where men toiled and died and thence on the backs of Indians and mules and other beasts of burden such as English slaves, to be assembled in forts and heavily guarded go-downs near the harbours for shipment eastward in the summer of 1591.

They had to cross this year; and Elizabeth was determined that they should not win through to Spain.

In March Sir Richard Grenville, who had lately returned to the West Country from his estates in Ireland, was summoned 'to make his repair to Her Majesty'. Arriving at the Court, he learned that he was appointed Vice-Admiral of a squadron that was to lie in wait in the vicinity of the Azores. Lord Thomas Howard was to command, with his flag in the *Defiance*; and to Grenville was given the *Revenge*.

8

I

At Flores in the Azores Sir Richard Grenville lay,
And a pinnace, like a flutter'd bird, came flying from far away:
'Spanish ships of war at sea! We have sighted fifty-three!'
Then sware Lord Thomas Howard: ''Fore God I am no coward;
But I cannot meet them here, for my ships are out of gear,
And the half my men are sick. I must fly, but follow quick.
We are six ships of the line; can we fight with fifty-three?'

Tennyson
(The *Revenge*: A Ballad of the Fleet)

Grenville turned from that square of sunlight and spoke softly into the gloom of the Great Cabin.

'Your zeal does you credit – if you needed any, in my eyes. But they'll come; *and* find us more than ready for them!'

He smiled at the sudden pleasure in young Gawdy's face; a moment ago the lad had been downcast, suggesting dismally that the Spaniards might already have slipped by, or – almost as bad, a postponement instead of a cancellation – be not coming in this season after all.

The sunlight, pouring through that single open port, stabbed into the cabin's greyness like a sword of fire, drawing smaller sparks of brilliance from silver ornaments on the heavy, oaken chest.

'You'll have your action, Philip. Enough to fill a dozen letters to that brother of yours, and make him green with envy!'

'To that, sir – amen!' Philip Gawdy spoke with feeling. He was the younger son of a younger son, and he'd joined the squadron as a gentleman-volunteer, delighted to be taken by Sir Richard (who was kin to Philip's uncle Anthony) and eager to make his mark and fortune. Perhaps he would – if the *flota* came.

His elder brother, Bassingbourne, had arranged his own affairs by marrying an heiress, three years ago: Philip knew that his own hopes of success lay chiefly in the rapier at his side and in the *Revenge* being in the right place at the right time.

She lay anchored now close off the north-west coast of Flores, closer in than the other ships, who had finished their rummaging (lightening the ships, then removing the old, foul ballast and scrubbing out and fumigating the holds and stores before embarking fresh, clean gravel from the shore) in the last day or two and moved out into clearer water where the stench of sickness from the land was less nauseating, and where the wind was more constant, less deflected by the tall shape of the bright green island. But the wind, being from east-south-east, still carried the taint of sickness in it from the land. There, rough canvas shelters in lines and groups on the lower slopes protected the stricken seamen. Fever (typhus, or ship-fever) had come suddenly, and spread as fast as plague. The *Nonpareil* had been sent back to England because she was so ridden with it, and the *Bonaventure* had been so short-handed that she had not enough men fit to handle her mainsail. To bring her crew to somewhere near full strength it had been necessary to take twenty men out of a barque of Sir Thomas Cary's, and scuttle the barque. But more had fallen sick since then, and none of the ships had a full crew, or near it. Ashore there, men were dying, a few men every day, sometimes as many as a dozen. Supplies were low, the victuallers in ballast and high in the water; throughout the squadron the men's rations had been cut to 'six men upon four', which meant six men sharing food for four. Except for such food as could be had in the islands – and that was little, except for fish – most of the stores were mouldy. Of beer, the ration being laid down as one gallon for each man on every day, there was none.

Gawdy was aware that his chances of achieving fame and fortune, or at any rate of winning either on this voyage, depended also on his finding favour in the eyes of Sir Richard Grenville and Lord Howard. So far, affairs had gone well indeed, Sir Richard showing him nothing but courtesy and consideration; and this over a period of five months away from England, a period which had included storms and near-dismasting, sickness and this long, increasingly tedious vigil. Any man's temper might by now have been short; and Grenville had the reputation of a martinet and hell-raiser, for savage moods and an uncontrollable temper. Ralph Lane, Grenville's second in command on the Virginia expedition fifteen years earlier, had complained of 'his intolerable pride and insatiable ambition'; but then, Grenville had been obliged at one stage to threaten Lane with hanging, and that could not have made for love between them.

Grenville had turned away, his profile etched black against that square of brightness. Gawdy saw again the high forehead, the strong, straight nose, a chin that jutted into the point of a carefully trimmed beard. He remembered the qualms and fears he'd had on first seeing this man whom the Spaniards – and the Azorians – hated and yet in front of whom it was reckoned foolhardy to mention the name of Francis Drake; seeing for the first time that appearance of fierce energy held in tight, uncomfortable control, that blaze of ruthlessness when the eyes turned to stare and question; seeing the man and remembering the stories, Gawdy had wondered, suddenly and prematurely homesick for his quiet Norfolk countryside, why he'd not stayed at home or sought a berth with Frobisher, or Drake ... Well, there was that distant kinship. And Frobisher had no command at present; nor had Drake, whose recent attempt on Lisbon had fizzled out in failure.

In any case, after that first heart-stopping interview when those dark, shrewd eyes had seemed to bore a path into his very soul, Gawdy had met only kindness and a consideration that was not much short of fatherly.

'Your company for a turn on deck, Philip?'

'Gladly, sir.'

He followed close behind as Grenville walked for'ard and pushed aside the canvas flap in that temporary bulkhead; beyond it, a smaller section of the Great Cabin had been divided into accommodation for Martin Langhorne, the soldier who was Grenville's Captain, and for Gawdy. Langhorne

11

wasn't there now. Gawdy followed the Vice-Admiral as he passed through the cramped, screened-off space (Langhorne's quarters on this starboard side, and his own to port) and by way of another canvas doorway to the tiller flat where the whipstaff stood lonely and unattended, held central by great straps secured to the deck on either side of the hole it passed through. This was the steering position. Farther down, below this deck which they were crossing, the whipstaff was hinged in a leather socket, and below that its foot was joined to the end of the great helm; so pushing the top of the whipstaff to one side or the other moved the helm in the opposite direction.

Just for'ard of the whipstaff stood the binnacle; and not much more than a foot abaft it was what seemed to be a timber supporting pillar, but was in fact the lower part of the mizen-mast; it pierced deck-head and deck and was stepped one deck below. (Mainmast and foremast, being very much heavier and carrying a great deal more sail, extended right to the bottom of the ship.) The mizen-mast here provided a convenient back-rest for the helmsman when in fine weather the whipstaff could be handled easily.

Light poured down into this flat from a small cowled opening in the deck above, just over where the helmsman's head must come. Through this aperture were passed helm orders from the quarter-deck – during normal sea watches they'd come from a quartermaster, at other times directly from the master.

Grenville's hand rested lightly on the smooth wood of the whipstaff as he passed it and set foot on the lowest of a flight of wooden stairs that rose from here to daylight; to be precise, to a sloping hatchway giving access to the half-deck. Here sunlight met them solidly; and the noise and bustle of the ship's company at their work came almost as a surprise after the calm and quiet they had left behind them in the Great Cabin. Down there, there had been only echoes of voices, and distant thuds and other sounds, muted by the heavy timber of the ship's construction; here was noise and movement, commands and hails, the squeaking of sheaves as gear that had been landed during the rummaging was

12

hoisted back aboard and struck down into the holds and store-rooms.

Here on the half-deck, Langhorne leant at ease against the bulwark on the port side while Bain, the Corporal, drilled a squad of musketeers. Seeing Grenville, the Corporal called his men to attention and Langhorne, straightening his tall and languid frame, doffed his hat with elaborate courtesy.

Grenville was bareheaded, and he wore no doublet, but a sleeveless jacket of green velvet over a shirt of white silk with heavy bunches of cambric at the throat and cuffs. He nodded at the Captain, and moved on past him, walking for'ard to look down into the ship's waist where the hard work of the forenoon was in progress. Philip Gawdy followed, exchanging greetings with Langhorne; the two had become good friends since they had first met, a few months ago, on this very deck. Last night the pair of them had shared with Grenville a gallon or more of the Vice-Admiral's quite excellent Rhenish wine; it had been part of the cargo of a Lubecker they'd captured soon after leaving Plymouth. She'd been bound for Spain, that hulk; Grenville had put a prize crew in her and sent her into Falmouth, after he'd relieved her of a few casks of this wine and sundry other items of more immediate interest than her main cargo, which was timber to the value of several thousand pounds. She'd proved easy enough to take, but *Revenge* had earned her by riding out a storm of considerable violence, between Scilly and Ushant, while Lord Thomas Howard with the rest of the squadron had lain in the shelter of Falmouth. (Grenville had made no comment when he'd heard of that, though his expression had been eloquent enough.)

But after the storm, which had been Gawdy's first frightening experience of the violence of the sea, when he had been writing a letter to his brother Bassingbourne, the Vice-Admiral had condescended to pen a note in its margin in his own hand; he informed the senior Gawdy that Philip's conduct was exemplary; that 'no sickness, danger nor fear, nor extremities of weather, mutiny or other peril' could provoke the young gentleman-volunteer from his duty. Philip had been delighted, imagining the impression those few words from such a famous hand would make upon his comfortable, land-bound brother; but in truth what had delighted Grenville had been the lines with which Gawdy had ended the main part of his letter. He'd written: 'the most of us like lions that have been almost famished for want of prey, or rather like a bear robbed of her whelps . . .' It was exactly how Grenville felt, and had felt before, and from that moment he'd warmed to the younger man.

Now they stood looking down into the ship's waist. Down there the hatches were open and men joked or swore, according to their temperaments, as they sweated at the ropes and tackles. Casks and cases, chests and sacks; among those gangs of seamen the Cooper worked, fitting new hoops on damaged barrels, inspecting with particular care each newly-filled water cask before allowing the Boatswain's party to lower it after the others into the bowels of the ship. The waist deck, on which three-quarters of the ship's crew were gathered about one task or another, was no more than thirty feet long and about the same in width, so that the scene, from here where they were standing, had a look of wild confusion. The steward was there, thrusting about among the gear with his two assistants, checking lists and registers; and the Gunner, who was apparently in a rage over something the Boatswain had done or not done, or perhaps said; Gawdy leaned forward, over the low bulwark above the cub-bridge head, and strained his ears for some clue to the cause of the dispute. All around them, men were grinning at their work.

Grenville frowned. 'What's amiss?'

Gawdy turned back to him. 'The Gunner wished to have his shot aboard last of all, sir, so that some could be distributed to the lockers at once and not all of it sent down first to his store. The Boatswain's crossed him by striking it down before the rest.'

Grenville nodded. 'He's right. If the Spaniards came now, I'd sooner have shot in the lockers than in the hold. Be pleased to step down there and call them both.'

Gawdy rattled down the ladder to the waist deck, and forced himself into the crowd of men at work. Mostly they

14

were of his own age, and less; mariners – trained men – and younkers, who could work only under supervision and on the simpler tasks. The older men – the sailors – were on the fo'c'sle and elsewhere, employed on more skilled tasks such as befitted their age and experience.

The two officers, both thick-set, bull-necked and now red in their faces with anger, still cursed each other; the Gunner with his short, thick legs planted well apart and fists bunched at his sides as he leant forward to bellow recriminations and abuse at the other; while the Boatswain, pretending to be entirely occupied with the work of his gangs at the lines and tackles, had turned away and only threw insults sporadically over his shoulder.

'Boatswain!' Gawdy was shouting as loudly as he could to make himself heard over the general din; the Boatswain turned, and, embarrassed, touched his hat. Gawdy nodded to the Gunner, then. 'And you, Master Gunner. The Commander, please.'

Their eyes followed the jerk of his head, and both of them stiffened when they saw Grenville up there, watching. There was a clear path now, back to the ladder, and they followed him, one behind the other. Gawdy ran straight up it to the half-deck, but Grenville's cold tones halted the others at the ladder's foot, where they doffed their hats.

'Boatswain. When this deck's cleared, you'll give my Gunner as many of your hands as he may ask for, to have that shot quickly where it should be.'

The Boatswain dropped his eyes. 'Aye, sir.'

'Master Gunner. If my officers so demean themselves as to abuse their fellows before the men, they'll be levelled down, others appointed in their place. D'you hear?'

'Your pardon, sir.' The voice was Devonshire, the man from Bideford. He'd sailed before with Grenville.

Sir Richard turned aft as musket butts clattered to the deck and Langhorne shouted loudly, pointing upwards over the ship's side, 'She closes to board! There, to larboard – clear her yards!'

The men flung themselves down behind the bulwarks on that side, aiming their muskets up into the rigging of an imaginary enemy, panting as they squinted along the long, heavy barrels. But the Corporal still stood behind them, as erect as if he was on parade, and Grenville, passing, touched him on the shoulder and remarked to Langhorne, 'This fellow's done for!' There was a growl of laughter from the kneeling men, and Grenville continued aft to the next ladder, a short one that led up from half-deck to quarter-deck.

That after deck, the crown of the poop, was deserted, though it was still wet from the Swabber's recent attentions. Right aft, on the very stern of the ship, was the roundhouse, the quarters of the Master. He'd be in there now, Pennyfeather, no doubt occupied with his charts and tables. The Master was the most able and experienced seaman in a Queen's ship; he needed to have served before the mast and to have performed the duties of every officer in the course of his career; then to have perfected his knowledge of the compass, the card, tides, time, wind and the reckoning of the ship's way; with these matters locked in his brain, and with formal commendations to the four principal officers of the Navy, he needed a warrant from Trinity House before he could be appointed a master in Her Majesty's fleet. It was on him the Commander relied for the navigation and handling of the vessel; since many commanders were no seamen, but soldiers or courtiers, they had need of a man who knew his trade.

Pennyfeather had seen them from the window of his roundhouse, and now he came to greet them.

'Good day, Sir Richard!' He nodded at Philip. 'Mr Gawdy.'

'Good day, Master. But I can't love this wind.'

'Nay, sir. While it holds, we'll see no treasure fleet; we can be sure of that!'

'Yet—' Grenville turned, and leant on the bulwark, staring out across ruffled water towards the other ships where they rode at anchor, and, from there, due west at that expanse of ocean – empty still, after the months of waiting. This island, Flores, with the smaller one called Corvo close to the north of it, was the westernmost of the Azores group.

'Yet – something tells me we'll be at them soon.' He laughed, and clapped a hand on Gawdy's shoulder. 'Then this young warrior will be satisfied at last. Night after night he charms us with his lute, but the music he pines for is that of guns!'

'Ay.' Pennyfeather stared shrewdly into Grenville's eyes. 'That do we all, Sir Richard; though some may more than others.'

Grenville had been looking idly down at the water; his head jerked up and his mouth was hard as he glanced quickly at the Master. But those sailor's eyes were hooded, now, the broad face bland, as expressionless as a piece of oak.

'No doubt,' murmured Langhorne, 'the fellow had some meaning. Sir Richard's known to be of a warlike disposition. Certainly he's not a man to cross, as Master Pennyfeather should know – and may know better presently, if he doesn't control his tongue!'

Langhorne and Gawdy were alone, leaning on the larboard bulwark of the half-deck. Grenville had gone ashore, to inspect the sick and talk with the squadron's chirurgeons who were ministering to them. He had not wished for company, but added that he might well be gone some hours, as he intended afterwards to climb the hill – as he had put it, 'to breathe clean air'.

As Langhorne spoke, he leaned out over the sea, looking towards the bow to see the Liar at work scrubbing the ship's side just beyond the break of the fo'c'sle. The man worked on a plank suspended from above by ropes that he'd secured to cleats inboard before descending. The ship had, by custom, two cleaners; the Swabber, whose permanent task it was to keep the inside of the vessel sweet, and the Liar, who was responsible for the outside and held his job only for seven days. Each Monday forenoon the first man caught in the act of telling a lie of any sort became the new week's Liar, and was proclaimed such before the mast at noon by

17

one of the Boatswain's Mates piping for attention and crying for all to hear 'A Liar! A Liar!' And a filthy job it was, for every time that a man had the need to relieve himself it was over the ship's side that he did it.

Langhorne pulled himself back, and added, 'He killed his first man before he was of age.'

'Sir Richard?'

'Yea. A brawl, in a London street. He ran him through.'

'But then, what—'

'A Queen's pardon within hours . . . I dare say the fellow gave him cause – and there were others in it too. But his temper's not slow, my dear Gawdy. It's not slow.'

Gawdy's spirits sank. Not because this story, which he'd not heard before, disappointed him in his estimate of Sir Richard Grenville: the reverse. He'd realized that he himself, during the years in which he and his brother had idled about the Inns of Court – years spent to no purpose other than that he'd learnt to play the lute – could no more have brought himself to kill a man in the street than he could have purchased the Tower of London. There was this difference between himself and Sir Richard Grenville, the difference that made Grenville a man of action and decision not by chance or favour or by willing himself so but by something in the blood, the force of his own character and kind; while he, Philip Gawdy, could hope for a stroke of fortune or a degree of fame by clinging to the service of one like Grenville, but never – as lately he had imagined he could – become that sort of man himself. Lately, conscious of the Vice-Admiral's approval, he'd seen himself as forming in the same mould. The mould didn't fit and never would.

'It surprises me,' mused Langhorne, turning his back to the bulwark and resting his long arms out along its top, 'that he should go walking alone in these islands, without attendants. He must know the natives hate him for what he did here only five years back. If I were he, I'd take a company of soldiers at my heels!'

'He sacked the place.' Gawdy shrugged. 'They fear him, more than hate—'

'Both, and there's little difference. But he'd been on the

18

second voyage to Virginia, in the New World. Placed men there to build a settlement, the year before, with Lane as Governor – as you'll recall? His second voyage was to their relief, with stores. But the settlers had come to grief and bloodshed with the Indians, and when Sir Richard's squadron dropped anchors at Roanoke there were no settlers there to greet him. That'd be bad enough – but it was Francis Drake who'd embarked them! So it's not surprising his temper had not much cooled when he touched here in the Azores on his way back to England; and these people suffered for it!'

Gawdy stared at him coldly. 'The Spaniards were here in occupation, were they not? And England at war with Spain? Is it necessary for Sir Richard to be out of sorts, do you suggest, before he performs his duty?'

'Oh, I'll agree – no need for excuses! Yet – they call him devil, hereabouts or rather, the Devil's kin.'

'But they're savages, no better than the Indians you spoke of! How do they live, what do they do? Not a good alehouse in twenty leagues; they're Papists to a man and they'd sell any one of us to the Inquisition for the price of a loaf of bread!'

'But speaking of excuses – as we *were*—' said Langhorne, after a pause, 'there's a story I can tell you that's another priceless feather in Sir Richard's hat. Or have you heard it – how he took the *Santa Maria*?'

Gawdy shook his head and Langhorne smiled, glad of the chance to tell it. 'It was on his return from that first voyage to Virginia – in 1585. You know he led that venture, and that it was in fact his cousin's, I mean Sir Walter Ralegh's, and Ralegh who gave Sir Richard the command. Well, he'd left his colony on Roanoke Island, and started homeward. But he – in the *Tiger*, of 140 tons – was separated by foul weather from the others of his squadron, the *Lion*, the *Elizabeth* and others, and came up astern of the galleon *Santa Maria*, which had also been separated from some *flota* bound for Spain out of San Domingo. And when the Spaniards see Sir Richard's ship, they regard him as one of their long-lost friends, and they shorten sail for him to come up closer. When the *Tiger* draws near, the Spaniard fires a gun to greet her!'

19

Langhorne chuckled; then he went on, 'Taking the salute in good spirit, Sir Richard orders his Master to turn the ship athwart the wind, presenting her length to the Spaniards, and he gives 'em his answer in a full broadside that brings down yards and cordage and kills half a dozen of the men on her decks. She tries to run, but he's crippled her, and she heaves-to instead. Now Sir Richard decides to board, but in the still unruly sea his Master is unwilling to lay *Tiger* alongside. And she has no long-boat, since it was left to be used by the men on Roanoke; all they have is a weak, crude thing made hurriedly out of planks. Well, Sir Richard being the man he is – and God bless him! – takes men with him in this cockle-shell, and they approach the Spaniard, and the boat – if it can be called a boat – smashes into pieces the moment it touches the *Santa Maria*'s side; so that he and his followers leap aboard her wet to their skins and lucky to have not drowned!'

Both men laughed, and Gawdy asked, 'He brought her home?'

'Ay. Stayed in her himself, and took her into Plymouth, passing through an even worse storm on the way and losing the *Tiger*, which put into Falmouth knowing nothing of their Commander's fate. But d'you see, England was not at war with Spain, and Sir Richard was called to account for this prize and the prisoners in her. Well, the words he wrote were these, or near enough, as I recall them: "On my way homewards I was encountered by a Spanish ship, which assaulting me and offering me violence, thank God, with safety of myself and all my company, after some fight I overcame and brought to England with me; her lading is such and such . . ." '

Grinning, Langhorne asked the younger man, 'D'you think, Gawdy, we'll be assaulted, *please* God, by some predatory treasure ships?'

* * *

Now half-way up the long, steep rise he paused and

looked back, his line of sight passing above the tents where in the last hour he'd inspected the sick and discussed matters affecting them with the ships' doctors – chirurgeons – and resting on the green and white upperworks of *Revenge* where she lay close inshore, from this viewpoint just to the left and closer in by a cable's length than the others of the squadron. She was the only one with that green paint on her; the others were chequered black and white, except for Vavasour's ship, the *Foresight* of 300 tons, which had light-blue instead of the black or green. Farthest to the right were the six victuallers, and with them the barque *Ralegh*; then, spread in a neat line and riding with their bows to their cables and to the east wind, like hounds straining at their leashes, so that from here they were in profile, was Lord Thomas Howard's *Defiance*, Captain Fenner's *Lion*, the *Bonaventure* under Captain Cross; these were all galleons of about 500 tons. Then came *Foresight*, and at the end of the line Captain Duffield's little *Crane*, of only 250 tons.

He looked at *Revenge* again. Figures which from here looked as small as puppets were at work around her mainmast; they'd lowered the yard almost to the deck and unlashed the mainsail, and Grenville could guess more than see that they were engaged in securing a bonnet to the foot of the course. Well, this wind was light enough; if news came suddenly of the *flota* they'd need that full spread of canvas, they'd need every square foot of it that could be mustered.

Pennyfeather knew his business, and did his job without having to be told or urged. No doubt, thought Grenville sombrely, he trades on that, on his own value, drawing courage from it for those sly, two-edged remarks . . .

But *Revenge* was in any case the best ship, for sailing qualities, in all Her Majesty's fleet. Of 500 tons' burden, she was classed as a ship 'of the middle sort', and being nearly one hundred feet long and thirty-two in the beam she was of true galleon proportions. She lay snug and low in the water with a depth-in-hold (from main-beam to keelson) of seventeen feet. She was three-masted, and fully rigged carried only six sails (mainsail, main-topsail, fore-sail and fore-topsail, mizen and spritsail) lacking the topgallants with which some newer and refitted vessels were now provided.

Her masts and yards weighed 17 tons and 7 hundred-weight, and the guns of her main armament, all below decks and in two tiers, 47 tons.

There were 34 of these guns: 2 demi-cannon, 4 cannon-periers, 10 culverins, 6 demi-culverins, 10 sakers and 2 falcons; and in recent years she had already used them well, and to the Spaniards' cost.

She'd been built at Deptford by Sir John Hawkins (*Revenge* was the prototype, now, for newer galleons) and launched there in 1577. Her career had been marked at intervals by mishaps and near-disasters; in 1586 she grounded at Plymouth, and before that came near to wrecking on the Irish coast, and there'd been other accidents. But she'd carried Francis Drake's flag against the Armada in 1588, and taken there her share of honours. (She'd been first engaged with Don Juan Martinez de Recalde's galleon *Santa Anna*; and later the vast *Nuestra Senora del Rosario*, carrying Don Pedro de Valdes who was the Commander of the Andalusian squadron, had struck to her. Then after the battle off the Isle of Wight and the fireship skirmish off Calais, it was *Revenge* who'd led the chase northwards, herself engaging the Duke of Sidonia in his towering flagship the *San Martin*.)

More lately she'd carried Drake on his expedition to Lisbon, and though the expedition had failed the Spaniards had felt her broadsides in Corunna, which Drake had first, and unwisely, attacked. On the way back to England she'd sprung a leak, and come near to drowning him!

But Drake had no command now, no deck beneath his feet. He had reached heights of success and fame too dizzy to allow for failure, and the Queen – or the Lord Admiral; but it came to the same thing – was permitting him to rest ashore in his splendid house, Buckland Abbey, near Plymouth.

* * *

Grenville turned from the prospect of the squadron and the sea, and climbed higher, towards a low wall of turf, grassed over, where he had often sat before.

Buckland, he thought. Well, Drake has my house – I have his ship!

Buckland Abbey had been bought by the old Sir Richard, this Grenville's grandfather, who had been Marshal of Calais and from whom this present Sir Richard had inherited – his father, Roger Grenville, having drowned at Spithead when the *Mary Rose*, of which he was Captain, turned over and sank there in 1545. This Sir Richard, now Vice-Admiral, had been three years old when his father drowned. But in manhood he had reconstructed Buckland, making it not only habitable but a place to be proud of and to love, and indeed he had loved it as well as he did his houses at Bideford and Stowe. In that great abbey he'd laid the plans, between 1570 and 1574, for a projected voyage to the South Sea, to discover *Terra Australis*, to circumnavigate the globe. But Her Majesty withheld the letters patent; he must first perform certain service for the Earl of Essex, in Ireland; and when that was done, a year later, for fear of offending Philip of Spain the Queen forbade his going. So he sold his ships – all but the *Castle of Comfort*, for which he had some private uses in the Channel – and three years later Francis Drake was permitted to embark on a voyage with the selfsame plan and object, only with the difference that by now the Queen did not care how deeply Philip might be hurt, so that Drake's was a voyage of plunder as well as of exploration. He came back the nation's hero and the Queen's favourite, and a rich man too, and after Grenville had sold Buckland to two intermediaries he learned that in fact he'd sold to Francis Drake, who had made *his* voyage, and a fortune, and glory – even history – with it . . .

Sir Richard rose to his feet, and glancing at the position of the sun decided he would walk a little way, for an hour or so, perhaps, before returning on board *Revenge*. By that time she should be ready and in order, and Pennyfeather could shift her out to lie with the others where the air was cleaner than inshore and where the wind waited ready to fill those sails at once when it was needed, when the *flota* came.

Well, he was nearly fifty years of age. In his early twenties – soon after he'd married Mary St Leger – he'd fought as a soldier in Hungary, against the Turks; and his first son, Roger, whom he had named after his own father, had died in infancy while he was still abroad. Then he'd gone to serve in Ireland, and later as a sheriff in his own West Country, he'd put down and crushed for good and all the embryo of a Papist revolt against the Queen's religion. Then – Justice of the Peace, although they'd hauled him up in Court, Richard Grenville, on charges of piracy, alleging illegal activities by his ship the *Castle of Comfort*! But that had been of little account. William Hawkins, brother of the Navy Treasurer himself, the Mayor of Plymouth and the Lieutenant of Portsmouth – these and many other honourable men had faced similar charges in those years. Sir John Killigrew, even, who was himself the Chief Commissioner for Piracy, and charged with its suppression! And into *his* affairs it was none other than Sir Richard Grenville who'd been appointed to inquire!

Then came the voyage to Virginia, commanding his cousin Sir Walter Ralegh's expedition. Thereby, in 1585, Grenville had planted the first settlement of Englishmen in America; 300 men he'd left there, to build a fort and establish a bridgehead in the New World. But in the next year he returned with supplies and reinforcements, only to discover that the colonists had been taken off, only a week or two before.

The man who'd taken them was Francis Drake . . .

Later, planning a third voyage to Virginia, Sir Richard had five ships ready and stored when, with the country in fear of a descent by the armadas of Spain, he received orders to remain in England with his ships and hold them 'in readiness to join with Her Majesty's Navy as he shall be directed hereafter'. But that further direction, when it came, was to send his ships to serve under Sir Francis Drake, and himself to remain ashore to assist in organizing the coastal defences of Devon and Cornwall . . .

They were fine ships, those which he'd been obliged to hand over to Drake's command: the *Dudley*, the *Virgin God Save Her*, the *Tiger* (in which he'd sailed to Virginia), the *St Leger* and the *Golden Hind*. Sir Richard's second son, John Grenville, had been captain of the *Virgin God Save Her*, and the *Golden Hind* had brought to Drake his first intelligence of the Spaniards' coming.

Well, he'd not questioned the order, or delayed in obeying it. He had never questioned or disobeyed an order in his life. He was a Queen's man, and a Grenville. Duty was to God, and to Her Majesty, and after that to yourself and to the name you bore. In that, your duty was to add to your estates and revenues, to increase the security and influence of those who came after and were yet to come; and to add to the honour of that name.

The Vice-Admiral paused on the crest of the ridge, just before he went out of sight of the island's northern coast-line; he looked back, down at the sea and at *Revenge*. The main yard was up again, now, the sail a neat parcel along it, and those tiny figures were at work on the fo'c'sle where the fore-sail yard had been lowered to within a few feet of the bulwarks. He stared down at her, at her neat compactness, and as he looked he felt a sudden, quite unheralded surge of pure excitement; not foreknowledge, because there was no cause that he could name to account for that quickening of his pulse and heartbeat, that blaze of exultation; it was a sudden sense of gladness and purpose that made him want to shout aloud, loud enough for Drake to hear at Buckland 1,200 miles away: *You have my house; by God, I have your ship!*

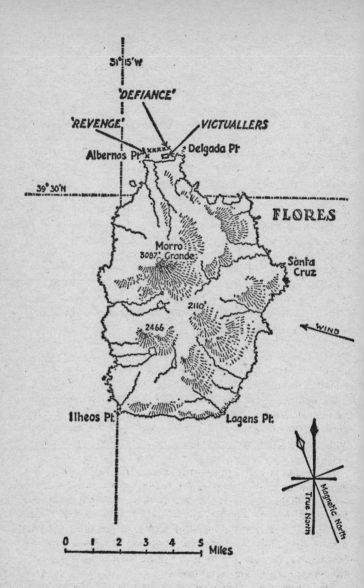

II

Gawdy was below, composing yet another of those letters of which Langhorne was by now heartily sick. It was not the frequency of the letter-writing that annoyed him, for that was entirely Gawdy's affair; it was having to read the things, or have them read to him, feeling himself obliged to smile or nod approval at the boyish enthusiasm which was their constant note. Sometimes he was even requested to add a few words of his own – as indeed Grenville had done, and with every sign of pleasure – to that frightful ass Bassingbourne of whom it was necessary, here on deck or down below during the long evenings in the Great Cabin, to hear so much so often! To Langhorne, Bassingbourne Gawdy (and what a name, for heaven's sake!) had assumed the appearance and attributes of some monstrous village idiot, lolling and drooling across those Norfolk pastures in the wake of his rich young wife – that paragon to whom young Philip paid assiduous court and compliments in every second line. But how any girl possessing both her senses and a fortune could possibly have consented to—

Langhorne checked himself. This was uncharitable; five months at sea in a ship 100 feet long – the boredom and the close, cramped quarters had taken their toll of patience and good fellowship. We need some action, he told himself, a battle, to clear the air and let the poison out of our souls!

He watched a flying-fish break out of smooth, dappled water and skim, and flop, and another farther out, this time a longer flight – or glide, for surely they never moved those fins when they were in the air? – and he told himself, Philip Gawdy is a splendid fellow, a man after my own heart; well, a splendid fellow, anyway; and that brother of his can't be blamed for having so much drivel addressed to him every time a pinnace leaves for home—

Well now, yes – that pinnace. It had been in his sight, in

the corner of his eye but not quite in his mind while he'd been thinking about the Gawdy family and watching idly the flights of fish. The pinnace – for that was what she was, he was studying her now and there was no doubt of it – had come in sight some while ago; at her first appearance she must have been north-east of Cape Delgada, perhaps three miles north-east of it, because now she was clearer to see and just about due north of the cape's extremity. About one mile off it, and the white canvas of her mainsail and spritsail gleamed in the sun as she came on with the wind behind her, steering due west across the top of the island's northern coast.

She'd come from the east, so she'd have no news of the treasure fleet. Now victuallers from that direction would have been more than welcome, in fact they were greatly overdue, and the opinion was that such victuallers as had been due to come must have been diverted instead to some other purpose, leaving this squadron to gnaw on whatever it had left. And a pinnace from the west: she'd be welcome too, likely to come from the ships which had been posted off Havana to report on the Spaniards' course when once they sailed. Well, this was neither of those things. This pinnace would bring dispatches, and rumours of this and that, perhaps some passenger (poor fool!) anxious to join the squadron. But worst of all, she might bring mails; mails from brother Bassingbourne which would be read and chuckled over and sighed at, and then read again, declaimed aloud, if not actually set to music on that damned lute!

More than once Langhorne had considered the possibility of arranging for an accident to befall that instrument. He had got as far as realizing that it would need to be weighted; being made of wood, it would otherwise float . . .

An entire shoal of flying-fish, a dozen or more, spurting out of the water and trailing drips that sparked in the sun-light as they dropped to mark behind each fish the track on which it flew; and *plop*, a dozen plops, but more already airborne, skimming the low, flat waves . . .

That pinnace was turning south, although she'd barely passed Cape Delgada. Langhorne watched her length shorten as her bow swung landward and the sails thinned to his view, spritsail bellied but no longer goose-winged, main-sheets hove in on her starboard side, flattening her mainsail to the wind that heeled her hard to starboard as she ran southwards on the port tack towards the anchored galleons. Langhorne lost sight of her now; then saw her again through the gap between the *Crane* and the *Foresight*, her bow-wave high and curling, whiter than any canvas. Now she was behind *Foresight*, and he was watching the next gap in the line of anchored ships when Gawdy's voice at his elbow shattered peace and concentration.

'What is it? Are we—'

Langhorne pointed, without excitement. 'A pinnace, from the Old World. From the east, in any case. She's running down towards us – or towards *them*. Dispatches, I dare say.'

'I see her!' Gawdy's voice held all the excitement that Langhorne's lacked. 'But are you certain she's not one of our own?'

The soldier glanced at him, then eastward at the sheltered anchorage right in the lee of that jutting headland. There lay the victuallers, and the *Ralegh*, and the three pinnaces with them; they were no farther offshore than *Revenge*, but at that end of the little bay they were in deeper water.

Gawdy had followed Langhorne's glance and absorbed the fact that none of their own pinnaces was at sea. This newcomer was a stranger, from some other squadron, perhaps even from England. The young man's face split in a wide smile. 'There may,' he said, 'be letters!'

'Ay.' Langhorne nodded gloomily. 'Indeed, it's not im-possible.'

The pinnace had lost its appeal for him. He left Gawdy to watch her approach, and turned to rest his back against the bulwark and to stare up at the bluish bulk of Morro Grande, vague and ethereal in the heat waves, the peak of it some four miles inland and 3,000 feet above sea-level. From Al-bernas Point, which formed the western extremity of the bay they lay in, a long, high ridge led up towards that summit; and half a mile to the east of that another ridge, less steep, which began in a small, round hill about a mile inland from the coast where the hospital tents were ranged, ran parallel and rose in the same way towards it. This was the ridge Grenville had climbed, crossing it just short of the hill where it gained height; the Vice-Admiral had passed over its crest, walking westward and out of sight, presumably down into the valley between those two long, southward-running spines. Langhorne had watched him, seen him rest there on the shoulder of the hill and then go on until he'd vanished suddenly. No doubt he'd be returning along that valley, along the bank of the stream that had its origins in the higher slopes of Morro Grande.

(In that stream they'd scrubbed and then refilled the water casks which were now stowed below, chocked and lashed in the for'ard hold below the cable locker. If no fresh stores came soon from England, they'd go hungry, here in the Azores; but they wouldn't die of thirst.)

He turned back, and could not see the pinnace. Gawdy told him, 'She's behind the – no, *there* she is! D'you see her? *There*.'

'Ay.' She was in sight again, between the *Bonaventure* and the *Lion*, holding her southwards course; it seemed she was almost on top of those resting galleons, running straight down towards the end of the line where Lord Howard's flagship lay. Langhorne noticed that all those decks were crowded now with watching men; there was a group on her quarter-deck, too, no doubt the Admiral with his officers. That reminded Langhorne of a question he'd been meaning to ask Gawdy since the morning of the day before, but forgotten whenever they'd been alone and he could have asked it. It was not an easy question to put, not one to put at all when there were others present.

'I wondered, Philip – I was thinking of it, and merely wondered – for what purpose Lord Thomas Howard summoned you, the evening before last. You dined with him, and – talked?'

Gawdy frowned, but he didn't move his eyes. 'Why, yes. But why'd you ask me that? He wanted company, and – but the Devil, why d'you ask?'

30

Langhorne shrugged. 'Curiosity; no more . . . But tell me, did he question you about Sir Richard?'

'He asked *after* him, and how we did, and so on, in politeness only; he treated me most courteously. Why, did you think—'

'Think? I'm a *soldier*, Philip, I know better than to *think*! Where's that pinnace?'

He'd get nothing out of Philip Gawdy, he might have known that. However pointed those questions of Lord Thomas's might have been behind their camouflage of courtesy and well-wishing, this lad would have been too naïve to recognize their purpose or to guess that the Admiral might be using him as a spy, as an informant in case anything which he might not like was brewing in the mind of his second in command. Howard was no seaman; but Grenville was, and besides that he was a man possessed of his own mind and spirit; and Grenville had this appointment, so it was rumoured, because his cousin Sir Walter Ralegh had declined the honour of serving under a man for whom his respect was limited. It was said, too, that Grenville had been the choice because his own experience of command and strength of personality could be relied upon to balance a lack of experience or decision in the Admiral. If these things which they said were true, or even partly true, then Howard would be a fool if he did *not* keep his eyes and ears open. The situation was not without its precedents.

That pinnace had crossed the view they had through the gap between the *Lion* and the *Defiance*, and as she vanished behind the cover of the flagship Langhorne looked aft, to his left, and saw that the news had spread, aboard *Revenge*; her waist and the fo'c'sle bulwarks on the port side were lined with men who found this arrival of a tiny, as yet unidentified craft a thing to watch and conjecture on, an event so small as to mean, most likely, nothing, but in any case an event of some sort in the long boredom of this mid-Atlantic watch. They lined the side, and chatted in groups, and no doubt that 'grapevine' of the lower decks already buzzed with rumours, one man's wild guess being weighted and embroidered with other fancies and with wishful or pessimistic com-

31

ments as it passed from group to group and man to man, resulting finally in firm belief and with consequent joy or resentment, depending on its final content. The murmur of the ship's company's voices had risen through a low, concerted growl to shouts which punctuated a steady roar.

Langhorne smiled, wishing that he could know how the talk went; he glanced back at the line of ships, but the pinnace was not in sight.

Over the left edge of the line, over the bare yards of the *Crane* and the *Foresight*, his eyes rested on the broad, flat summit of Caldeira on the island of Corvo, sister to Flores. It was some ten miles distant, east-north-east from this anchorage, and the edge of Caldeira was straight and sharp against the pale-blue sky. Beyond that edge, at a height of 2,500 feet, was the crater which held the lakes; he'd bathed in one of them – and regretted it within seconds of immersion – when some weeks ago he and Gawdy and some of the gentlemen in Lord Howard's entourage had been taken there by pinnace for a day of recreation. Only to think of it now made his bones begin to ache again from the exertion of the climb and the chill of that cold, clear water . . .

Gawdy was plucking at his sleeve. 'Here she comes, now! D'you see her?'

The Captain nodded. Excitement on the midships and for'ard decks was rising to a crescendo; even Pennyfeather had condescended to come out of his hutch – although he stayed near it, having noticed Langhorne and Gawdy at the for'ard end of the quarter-deck. The Master was a man who preferred his own company – afloat, at any rate – and Langhorne admired him for it. He admired too the man's obvious self-confidence, his quiet professionalism. Without men like Pennyfeather, none of these ships could be at sea.

Now the pinnace was knifing down between the bows of *Defiance* and the rocks which extended north and west of Delgada Point; she too had a seaman in command of her as she lanced that narrow gap between the flagship's cable and the rocks to port, the largest of them almost an island by its size and certainly no more than thirty yards off her beam as she passed it, still under full sail although as she came under the lee of Delgada her way had lessened so that she was upright in the water and her mainsail no longer taut though not quite flapping, at least so far as the eye could tell from this distance. She had passed and cleared *Defiance*; on her port side now were rocks surely almost close enough to touch, and immediately ahead of her in an impassible block were the victuallers and their consorts, only yards distant from her narrow bow: and she'd gone over, hard to starboard, the wind behind her now, her prow to the west and her course parallel to the coastline, between that and the anchored men-of-war.

Langhorne's hands gripped the top edge of the bulwarks as he leaned over, fascinated and intent. There was silence now on *Revenge*'s decks as every man watched, absorbed, and abruptly the pinnace went about, turning on her heel to starboard, towards the flagship and all the way round as her spritsail fluttered and crumpled and was dragged inboard and she turned into the wind, mainsail quivering, then backed; then main yard absorbed mainsail as it was triced up jacknife fashion leaving her under bare poles and all but stopped, but drifting still with the way she'd had before, drifting gently and with absolute precision to kiss the flagship with the larboard side of her length of forty feet. There on the *Defiance*'s decks men were ready to pass her the securing ropes.

At Langhorne's elbow, someone coughed loudly. The soldier spun round, startled, he'd heard no one approach. Both he and Gawdy stared in surprise which in politeness they quickly tried to hide. It was the Master – Pennyfeather – he'd come aft, unbelievably, to address them . . .

Having their attention, Pennyfeather coughed again more gently.

'Gentlemen, I'd say this. You may sail as long as I have, and then twice as long; and if in that time you should see a ship of any sort handled more sweetly – this side of heaven! – than you've seen this morning, then – why, I'd envy you!'

Langhorne, still thrilled by the sheer perfection of the manoeuvre he'd seen executed a few minutes ago, realized through overlaying surprise that to have walked a dozen paces and actually addressed two laymen on the subject of his own dedicated profession, Master Pennyfeather must have been moved indeed.

But the Master had not waited for any reply or comment. His back was already towards them as he stumped aft to re-enter the privacy of his round-house, that holy of holies where the back-staff and the astrolabe were the outward and visible emblems of all the mysteries at his command.

'Captain Langhorne, sir.'

The soldier turned, and Josiah Wenman, the Master Gunner, touched his hat. He growled, 'Captain, sir; I'd report the lockers shotted.'

Langhorne nodded, slowly. But with his eyes on Wenman's rugged and normally ruddy face, he was asking himself what could be the matter with the man. He was pale, and had a look of strain. In sudden alarm Langhorne thought, *The fever: has it got to him?*

'Are you strong, Master Gunner?'

'Strong enough, sir.' Wenman smiled uneasily. 'I'm not sick, if that's your meaning . . .' His eyes flickered away; that in itself was unusual enough.

Langhorne nodded, wanting to ask more but thinking of no way to probe beyond that grim, disturbed exterior. Wenman touched his hat again, turned for'ard and moved towards the ladder.

It had begun two hours ago when the Boatswain and his party had finished with that fore-sail and run the yard up two-blocks at the truck and belayed it there, and the Boatswain had come aft into the waist and asked Wenman gruffly, making it plain that he was obeying the Commander's whim and doing no favour of his own volition, 'Well then, my men's done with. How many'll you want?'

Wenman remembered how he'd stared back into that angry, half sneering face and told its owner, Daniel Sturgee,

34

'Why, every man jack of 'em! Every one, Dan! Ay, and two of your boys into the bargain, to work the shot-room!'

He'd been enjoying his victory as he'd said it; but he'd seen, in that moment, the Boatswain's smile, and a kind of worry had stirred for the first time in the back of his mind. But there'd been other matters to arrange, and he'd turned away to get on with them . . .

'Gun Captains, Quarter Gunners to your pieces!'

The shrill pipe had stilled their voices, and in the silence he'd yelled that order; these men grouped before him, now melting down into the hatch that led to the lower decks and holds, were his own people, all of them gunners. He turned now to Hardcastle and Rowan, his lieutenants, the Gunner's Mates.

'The deck lubbers'll do the hard work, lads. When I send 'em down, set a line of 'em along your decks – yours first, Will – close enough to pass shot hand to hand. We'll send out the shot as you call for it. D'ye follow me? Alec?'

They nodded, grinning. Wenman told them, 'Then take your decks, lads.'

They went quickly to the hatch: Will Hardcastle gaunt, walking stiffly, jerkily, as if his bones were badly joined, some of them too long for the frame they were supposed to fit: and Alec Rowan struttingly, a man for the women, this, proud of his youth and ability, cocksure – and that with reason! Josiah Wenman grinned, and turned to Robert Drax, the Yeoman of the shot-room.

'Well, Bob, you may open up. I've two seamen boys to work in there—'

He saw them, in that instant as he turned and stared up at the fo'c'sle break, at the solid knot of the Boatswain's party who were waiting there for their orders. A little apart from the rest stood Daniel Sturgee, and with him, with his hands resting on their shoulders, were the two boys.

'You wanted two, Joss. These do?'

Wenman froze. One of the boys was Wally Maine, an overgrown lout who'd be the better for a dose of hard work. The other was his own son, Jonno Wenman.

Joss remembered his wife's final, bitter words, spoken so quietly so the lad shouldn't hear them: 'You're a brute, Joss, you with your talk of building him up, making a man of him! He's too young, too small by half, you know it! You've no heart, Joss Wenman, not even for your own! You don't care for *nothing*, except your cannons!'

She'd been wrong, of course, but he'd been sorry for her in her grief; sorry, and quite unable to tell her that he had to get the boy away from the strings of her apron and into his own custody, into the company of men ... Well, the boy wasn't strong, or big; so he'd put him under the Boatswain rather than into his own department where the work was mainly below decks. Salt air had indeed done the boy good: only yesterday the Master Gunner had taken his son ashore for a walk and an afternoon's chat, and he remembered now that he'd smiled to himself in pleasure and approval as he'd imagined how Jane was going to have to eat her words when she saw this healthy, filled-out stripling ... Well, he was twelve years old, wasn't he?

Of course, the Master Gunner and most of the key men among the gunners had themselves served at sea as boys, and had done this shot-room job more than once, and survived it with no after effects other than a bit more muscle in their arms. It wasn't all *that* bad.

Only Jonno's mother had been right when she'd said he wasn't strong. He took too much after her, her with that weakness in the back, the spine; those headaches she complained of – or, more often, didn't ...

That was Jonno, Jane's boy, up there with his messmate Wally Maine; Boatswain Sturgee's hands gripped their shoulders and a smile parted the lips that framed those broken teeth. Smiling, he stared down at the Gunner.

Wenman knew perfectly well there was nothing he could do about it. He'd asked for two boys, and he'd got them. If he refused to let his son do this job – well, it was unthinkable. The other seaman boys, particularly whichever took his place, would make Jonno's life a hell for ever after. Josiah met his son's eyes and saw the trust in them, saw that the boy was happy in the thought that now he was going to do some work under his father's direction. *What would he be thinking in an hour's time?*

The Master Gunner held Sturgee's eyes for a long moment. Then he turned away, and shouted over his shoulder, 'Boys to the shot-room! Men to the gun-decks! *Move, now!*'

Each Gun Captain stood beside his own piece and locker; each Quarter Gunner had charge of his own section of the main armament; the two Gunner's Mates each commanded his own deck of guns. The Yeoman of the shot-room had opened up his store, which was itself the stern portion of the lower gun-deck, divided from it only by canvas screens which had now been pushed back out of the way.

(In the gun-room, the Master Gunner presided over his own Mess, which housed the senior men of his department. It was perhaps the most highly disciplined Mess in the ship, for its members – the Gunner's Mates, Quarter Gunners and Yeomen – were chosen and appointed by the Master Gunner, who could send any of them back to communal living before the mast if they at all displeased him.)

Into the shot-room went the two seamen boys. Their small size fitted them for work in that small space, and by custom this was a task for boys – though normally for those attached for gunnery duties – to pass up shot to the men who crouched above the hatchway. The Yeoman had only to point out to them which shot to hand up, and when, and to rally them with curses or blows when their arms and lungs began to weaken as the work progressed.

When all was ready and the line formed, shot began to stream out from its bulk stowage and along the decks to the lockers, boxes of heavy timber, one to each gun, fixed to the ship's sides between the gun-ports. The shot came in order of calibre and of the stations of the different types of gun; lockers were filled, in general principle, from for'ard to aft, and the lower deck before the upper one. As each locker was filled, the Captain of that gun would slam down his lid and shout 'No more!' Then, when Quarter Gunners had their sections of lockers filled, they'd bellow in the same way to the Gunner's Mate of that deck, who'd halt the stream of that calibre or divert it to another section. It was the particular art of the Mates to stop the flow at its source just before the lockers were exactly filled, so that men would not be left with shot in their hands which would have to be returned to the shot-room.

The first shot to come up was for the culverins, all of which, being in themselves heavy pieces, were on that lower deck; there were five on each side, two pairs for'ard of the great pillar of the mainmast where it ran solidly through from deck-head to deck (and down to its step above the keelson) and three pairs abaft it, the aftermost pair being in the gun-room Mess where the canvas bulkheads had been struck down out of the way of the work. The culverins were each twelve feet long and five inches in bore at the muzzle; they took seventeen-pound shot and they were the longest range guns in the ship – indeed, in the Navy.

With much less range, but greatly heavier in calibre, were the pair of demi-cannon. These too were on the lower gun-deck, one to port and one to starboard immediately abaft the mainmast. Thirty-pounders, their shot five inches in diameter, designed and used to pound and break enemy hulls. When they were done with, the boys in the shot-room gasped their relief; that was the heaviest shot finished, and the lower gun-deck shotted.

But in the larger calibres – and on the upper deck there were still the cannon-periers to be served – it was not only a matter of passing up single balls of 30, 24 and 17 pounds apiece, and dozens of each size, hundreds of some; a proportion of the iron that went to each locker was chain-shot and bar-shot, two balls joined either by a short chain or by two bars eyed together in the middle to give a certain flexibility to the whole and to facilitate loading. With these monstrosities the lads worked together, one lifting each of the linked balls, straining in unison to lift them to the level of the hatch, to those ever empty, waiting hands. Sweat poured down their faces and bodies until there was no part of them dry, and they gasped for air in that small, unventilated space where only rats might live in any sort of comfort; they gritted their teeth, groaned with the effort, panted like dogs, near-blind with the sweat in their eyes, wanting to scream and beg for relief and rest but knowing that if they did they'd be marked as weaklings and jeered at for the rest of the voyage by every man and boy aboard; and the shot, which was intended ultimately to shatter Spanish timbers, was well blooded from their own torn hands before it even reached the hatch.

But now it was the turn of the upper gun-deck. Shotting that lower deck had taken a good deal more than an hour. Josiah Wenman – he'd put the thought of his son as far out of his mind as he'd been able to, relegating it to a black cloud behind a hundred more immediate thoughts, only re-membering to keep himself well away from that shot-room hatch – redisposed the Boatswain's men, ordered the Gun Captains on that lower deck to stand easy, and when all was ready he turned to Alec Rowan and nodded briefly. Rowan muttered,

'That boy of your'n—'

'He'll be—'

'Not the build for it. You—'

'I'd no choice, Alec. You saw that, eh?'

'Ay. But Daniel Sturgee—'

'I'll kill him, if Jonno's hurt.' There was no apparent vehemence in the Master Gunner's voice. He held himself under rigid control and this had been a statement of fact, not a threat made in rage but a thing that might have been de-cided in the very moment he'd looked up and seen his son with that Boatswain's hand upon his shoulder.

Wenman's face was calm, anger showing only in the eyes. He raised one bushy eyebrow at Rowan. 'Periers, then?'

The Mate nodded. 'Periers it is. Then demi-culverins.'

The Master Gunner pushed himself upright, away from the mainmast against which he'd been leaning. He stepped around the end of the pin-rail, slotted and spoked with be-laying-pins where the main halyards were turned up; those ropes passed through square apertures in the deck above, close to the place where the mainmast pierced it. Wenman pushed himself past the port-side cannon-periers, resting his right hand on their round pommelions as he forced himself aft, pushing men aside, stooping to pass under the low beams of the deck above. Taller men were bent double, in these shallow 'tween-deck spaces. Wenman bellowed,

'Periers! Twenty-four-pound shot, now! Periers here, and lively!'

The four cannon-periers were amidships; short, light pieces, but wide-bored and throwing heavy shot. They were for short-range work, hammer-work; smaller versions of the demi-cannon down below. After them came demi-culverins, long range ten-pounders; a pair right for'ard comprised the bow-chase, two more right aft in the Wardroom (where the Boatswain, Chirurgeon, Boatswain's Mates, Quarter-masters, Corporal and Carpenter messed) made the stern-chase, firing through ports in the stern itself; and there were two more near amidships, only abaft the periers. But in the for'ard section of the upper gun-deck were also four sakers, long range six-pounders, junior members of the culverin family; and four more sakers stood between the mizen-mast and the stern-chase.

The ball streamed up from hand to hand, men grumbling, cursing softly as they passed the endless flow of rough-cast iron and the gunners watched with eagle eyes in case shot of one calibre should go in error into a locker meant for some other; and when this second deck was finished there were still the light guns on the decks above; two sakers in the for'ard part of the Great Cabin, and aft of them two port-pieces, man-killers of six-inch bore that fired grape-shot, ten pounds of it at each blast. In the fo'c'sle were two falcons, long three-pounders; and in the steerage, below the half-deck, four fowlers. These, with a three-inch bore, were the smallest cousins of the periers.

When all the lockers throughout the ship were fully shotted, the Master Gunner blew his whistle and dismissed all but his own men. He caught Rowan's eye, and jerked his head towards the stern; the Mate winked, solemnly, and headed aft towards the shot-room, beckoning two of the Gun Captains as he passed them.

With Hardcastle behind him, Wenman toured the gun-decks, peering briefly into every locker, exchanging a word or two with the gunlayers at their posts, sometimes stooping to examine the ropes of a gun's tackle. That done, he reported to Captain Langhorne; then on for'ard, and down to the powder-room, which was in the lower hold just abaft the foremast step, between the fore peak and the cable lockers. Here the Yeoman of the powder-room was ready for his chief's inspection of kegs and cartridges, linstocks, slow-matches, fire pikes and bombs.

While he was still down there, the two seaman boys had been dragged out of the shot-room by their shoulders and carried up to lie exhausted on the fo'c'sle deck, where buckets of salt water were poured over them to hasten their recovery. Maine had his eyes open, and rolled about, muttering and groaning and trying to sit up; but Jonno Wenman lay flat on his back and never moved. Alec Rowan knelt beside the boy, listening to the short, hard breaths; without turning his head he muttered to Robert Drax who crouched beside him, 'Not the build for such labour, he hasn't.'

Drax shook his head. 'The Chirurgeon—?'

'He'd not come, not for one boy that's short of breath. He's got prime men dying there ashore!' The Gunner's Mate rose slowly to his feet, still looking down at the unconscious boy. Abruptly, he changed his mind.

'It's worth a try. Ay, I'll ask for the long-boat. It's Boatswain Sturgee I've to ask – and I'll tell him why! You keep your eye on the lad, Bob.'

Wally Maine was sitting up, shaking his head like a dog that's just come out of water. Rowan stared at him.

'*You're* fit, then; so they're right, and the Devil looks after his own!' Maine grinned dutifully, and Rowan went on, 'Well, make yourself useful. Nip below and fetch a drink of clean water for y'mate here. Eh?'

Maine looked down at Jonno Wenman's pale face, at the closed eyes with that tracery of fine blue veins across their lids.

'Is he—?'

'No, he ain't. Lively now, boy – *water*!'

Maine staggered to his feet and set off drunkenly towards the hatch, shaking his head again in that curious way, holding his still oozing hands away from his body and opening and clenching them as he walked. Rowan turned back to Drax.

'You may get some drink into him, Bob. Do what you can while I'm gone.' His tone was almost pleading. He started away, but checked and turned back. 'When that youngster's fetched the water, Bob, send him to tell Joss Wenman.'

Langhorne watched a long-boat leave the flagship's side, oars tossed vertically, bowman erect; there were officers, or persons of consequence, in the stern. Langhorne had seen them climb down the ladder from the *Defiance*'s deck; now they'd taken their seats and from here made all one group with the boat's coxswain, and it was impossible to see any details of their appearance.

The oars fanned down as the bowman took his thwart, and a moment later the boat drove forward, oar blades biting water, throwing white; the long-boat was heading westward from the flagship, inside the line of other ships; but it wasn't possible to know yet whether it was on its way to one of those others, or coming here, to the *Revenge*. For either purpose, its course initially would be the same.

'News!' Philip Gawdy smiled his delight. 'News – from England! Why, it'll be like having messages from some other planet!'

Langhorne shrugged. 'That boat may be conducting gentlemen from the flagship to visit in *Bonaventure*.'

'I would say it had passed the *Bonaventure*—'

'Ay. Then to *Foresight*, or the *Crane*. But hold, Philip, and soon we'll know for sure . . . Well, I'll grant you it's not bound for *Foresight*.'

Gawdy told Langhorne, peevishly, 'I tell you, it's coming here. See how its course diverges from those others!'

He was right, and Langhorne slowly nodded. The boat's course was apparent, now, coming out clear of the line at anchor, well set on that half-mile of sheltered water which divided *Revenge* from the rest of the fleet. Langhorne felt the ship listing, as her company massed again along the port-side bulwarks, to watch the flagship's boat approach.

Gawdy muttered, 'There must be letters for us, or they'd not send so quickly!'

That boat's crew were uniformed; so the boat was Lord Howard's own, its men dressed alike at his personal expense. It was a custom among rich Captains, almost *de rigueur* for Admirals; but Grenville scorned it. Sir Richard, who lived in the strict manners and style of a gentleman and would have no food served in his Great Cabin on anything but silver dishes, no wine drunk out of anything but silver goblets, insisted that to put seamen into uniforms was to insult and demean them, bringing them to the level of flunkeys or door-keepers.

Langhorne turned quickly as footsteps padded towards him along the deck; the Boatswain, Sturgee, raised a hand half-way towards his hat, and halted.

'Your pardon, sir. Beg permission to send the long-boat inshore, to bring off the Chirurgeon. There's a boy for'ard needs his skill.'

'Fever?'

'Nay, sir.' Sturgee looked awkward. Langhorne frowned, wondering what was the matter with them all this forenoon. First Wenman, looking as if he'd suffered a miscarriage, and now this Boatswain with the air of a trapped felon!

'Young Wenman it is, sir. His father used him too hard in the shot-room, and by the look of him he's all but done for. If it were any other lad, sir—'

Langhorne snapped, 'There'd be some difference?'

'Nay, sir!' Sturgee looked confused as well as frightened. 'But he's not strong, sir, that's my meaning. A puny fellow for such labour—'

Langhorne's brain was working fast, this morning. He nodded grimly at the Boatswain. 'Young Wenman – one of *your* boys, is he not? So as the Commander gave you that order, you chose him for the task?'

His eyes narrowed, and the Boatswain's glance dropped,

confirming what had been no more than a shrewd guess. Langhorne's grunt was a sound of contempt.

'Ay, Boatswain, send in the long-boat; and my own compliments to the Chirurgeon, request he makes all haste.'

'Aye aye!' Sturgee turned, but another voice stopped him. Pennyfeather, who'd heard the conversation, came closer.

'Captain Langhorne. I'd not question your decision. But since there's a boat approaching from the flagship, should we not hold ours against some need of it? The Vice-Admiral being ashore?'

The Master was right. Langhorne thanked him, and told the Boatswain to call away the long-boat's crew and have them man their craft, but to hold it alongside at the waist on the starboard side.

Pennyfeather nodded. 'An excellent decision, Captain Langhorne.' A craggy smile lingered on the Master's face. He added, 'If I may say so, sir, it's a pity you chose to be a soldier!'

Langhorne, delighted at the compliment, grinned back. Himself well-born, though like Gawdy lacking much silver on the spoon, the approval and suggestion of proffered friendship from this man who'd made himself out of nothing but his own abilities was something to be prized. Langhorne liked both Pennyfeather and himself the better for it.

Gawdy broke into their amusement. 'That long-boat's near to us! There's Captain Strong in her, and a stranger. By the looks of him, a gentleman—'

'Ay ... I know him.' Pennyfeather's eyes were narrowed to slits as he stared across the gap of shining water; the boat was no more than fifty yards away. 'Captain Middleton, in her Majesty's service. He'll have brought that pinnace—'

'Then he's from England!'

'Nay, sir.' Pennyfeather barely glanced at Gawdy. 'I'm of the opinion Captain Middleton was with the Earl of Cumberland—'

'Whose squadron,' put in Langhorne sharply, 'is on the coast of Spain!'

'Ay.' The Master nodded. 'It was, when we last heard.'

Langhorne turned to Gawdy. 'Then we'll have news, it seems, not of England, but of Spain!' He seemed amused at Gawdy's obvious disappointment.

The long-boat's crew had tossed their oars, and a line from *Revenge*'s waist fell slanting across its bows. The bowman had shipped his oar and now he grabbed the line, taking up the slack hand-over-hand as the boat slewed in and bumped alongside; the crew grasped hold of the galleon's side, pressing their fingers into the crevices of the closed gun-ports, risking their blue-and-gold uniforms against those salt-damp timbers. The two officers were out of sight now as they climbed the port entrance ladder, where their boat had come to rest; the stranger came first, with Strong, who was Captain of Soldiers in the flagship, close behind him.

Langhorne and Pennyfeather, with Gawdy following more slowly, had rattled down the ladder from quarter-deck to half-deck; the visitors came up the lower ladder, from the waist, and it was on the half-deck that the parties met.

'Welcome, gentlemen.' Langhorne bowed.

Captain Strong bowed too. 'It's my honour to present Captain Middleton, from the squadron of the Earl of Cumberland. Captain Langhorne, Mr Gawdy, Master Pennyfeather ... Captain Middleton must speak urgently with Sir Richard Grenville—'

'Who's ashore.' Langhorne added, seeing their consternation, 'But our long-boat's ready alongside. I can take you to him quickly; or if you prefer it, send your message to him?'

Strong and Middleton glanced at each other; then Strong turned back to Langhorne and told him, 'Best take your boat and ours as well, so we can return direct to Lord Howard ... You're ready now, sir?'

'Ready.' Langhorne stepped forward; Middleton spoke to Pennyfeather.

'We met in Plymouth – a year ago?'

Pennyfeather inclined his head. 'Ay, Captain Middleton, we did.'

'Just so. Forgive this scant courtesy, Master, but time's

short and the Spaniards not far off. In your Commander's absence, I'd urge you to prepare for sea.'

Pennyfeather's blunt fingers scratched at his bearded chin. 'The treasure fleet, sir?'

Middleton shook his head as he moved away. 'Men-of-war, fresh from Spanish ports. Twenty galleons and more than thirty well-armed merchants. Well—' he turned, and followed Strong over that low bulwark on the port side of the waist, dropped expertly down the ladder into Lord Thomas Howard's long-boat as Strong snapped out an order to its coxswain.

On the other side of the waist-deck Langhorne had paused, listening; now he called to Pennyfeather, 'You'll make ready?'

'Aye aye.' Pennyfeather faced aft, roaring for the Boatswain. The morning's peace was shattered now by shouts and the noise of running feet, and Langhorne bellowed, 'Master Gunner! *You* there, fetch me the Master Gunner!'

'Here, sir!' Wenman had flung himself out of the hatch; he'd been below, placing his son in the gun-room, on his own cot. His hat was askew and he pulled it straight. 'Sir?'

Langhorne was already on the ladder above the boat. Head and shoulders over the bulwark, he told Wenman, 'Run out the upper tier of ordnance. Serve powder ... Ay, and the Corporal to break out muskets, ball and pikes. All lively, Master Gunner!'

He vanished on the last words, down into the boat; the other one, with Strong and Middleton in its stern-sheets, had already rounded the ship's stern and was half-way to the landing-place.

Pennyfeather had given his orders to the Boatswain, who'd rushed for'ard shouting for his Mates and Quartermasters; even now, the first men were swarming aloft to clear the yards. Pipes shrilled, and the ship was alive like an ants'-nest suddenly disturbed.

Pennyfeather, hurrying aft towards his round-house, looked out across the water at the flagship and those other galleons lying near her. Their decks, too, and their rigging,

46

seethed with men; and with a start of surprise the Master saw that they were already heaving in their cables.

The Dons, thought Pennyfeather, must indeed be close at hand ... And by the looks of it, Lord Howard doesn't wait for his Vice-Admiral!

III

So Lord Howard passed away with five ships of war that day,
Till he melted like a cloud in the silent summer heaven;
But Sir Richard bore in hand all his sick men from the land
Very carefully and slow,
Men of Bideford in Devon,
And we laid them on the ballast down below;
For we brought them all aboard,
And they blessed him in their pain, that they were not left to Spain,
To the thumbscrew and the stake, for the glory of the Lord.

Tennyson
(The *Revenge*: A Ballad of the Fleet)

Grenville's expression was more of surprise than of alarm,
and certainly their own feelings of urgency found no echo in
his voice or reflection in his eyes; they lingered coldly, now,
on the flushed face of Captain Strong, who'd finished his
explanation, imparted the full message from Lord Thomas
Howard to his second in command; Strong and Middleton
faced the Vice-Admiral squarely while Langhorne had
moved round to stand at his Commander's elbow.

Still silent, and having made no comment of any sort on
the news they'd brought him, he turned his back on them
and stared inland, narrow-eyed, apparently absorbed in the
study of that hill he'd climbed three hours ago . . .

From its shoulder, when unknown to him Langhorne had
been watching his movements from the deck of *Revenge*,
he'd walked down into that first valley and crossed its
stream and climbed again, westward over the next ridge and
then down to that other stream which like its brother started
high up on the converging slopes of Morro Grande; from
there the Vice-Admiral had gone on westward and up a
gentler incline until near the coast he'd stood to look down
on Gadella Island and the swirl of sea that broke across its

48

rocky edges and surged to and fro in violent foam through the narrow gap which divided it from Flores. The water was deep, on this western coast, the shore itself steep-to, the hundred-fathom line no great distance from the land.

He'd turned south, then, climbing towards an intermediate summit that lay back from the coast and half-way to the height of Morro Grande. Up there he'd rested, his back to the hillside and his face to the west where below him the Atlantic spread itself first in broken, frosted green with patches and whorls of lighter green and white and black where rocks lay awash or just below the surface but still quite visible from above; then past Fanaes Point and Monchique Island, beyond those final outposts of Azorian rock, there was only blue-black sea, all that vastness of it with only wind and sky for company. It was on that white-flecked sea that his eyes had rested, feeling indeed at rest in the sight of it but at the same time seeking, probing, wanting that glimpse of topsails that could only be of Spain and thus put finish to the months of waiting.

Months – *or a lifetime*? Grenville half frowned to himself, alone on that hillside with the Atlantic spread hugely at his feet. This was a feeling that lately had been growing in him: of having *waited* all his life, with everything that he had done being only interludes or stages or approaches to some climax which now was close at hand. Barely two hours ago he'd felt without warning or known reason that onrush of excitement, a sense of the imminence of some tumultuous moment of fulfilment.

But the sea was empty, placid, barely ruffled by the stroking hand of a gentle wind under the noonday sun; the great, smooth arc of the horizon was clear, as unbroken as it was unhazed. The islands and the now invisible English squadron possessed this stretch of ocean, and no Spanish ships could be here today to challenge their occupation of it.

All that had been day-dream, wishful thinking coupled with hard-tried patience ... Deliberately he quietened the excitement in his mind.

So he'd rested there, and, for an hour, slept; then, waking, suddenly aware of the passage of time, he recalled that by this afternoon the ship should be ready to move out and anchor with the others, that Pennyfeather would be awaiting his return and the command to weigh, to drift under topsails into the deeper water and there re-anchor in the line; he remembered, too, without pleasure, that tonight he was expected by Lord Howard to dine aboard the flagship.

Grenville rose slowly to his feet, once more examined carefully that great stretch of ocean in which the island of Flores had approximately the significance of an acorn in an exceptionally large meadow; once more frowned, and thought in sudden desperation, 'Another day: that at the least. But another week? A month?' Then, empty-handed, back to English winter, the provident management of estates and perhaps never again the chance to serve Her Majesty at sea and in the process win the honours which lesser men had come by easily and which chance had for years kept just beyond his fingertips?

Retirement? Comfortable old age? Respect too often tinged with sympathy?

He told himself quickly, '*No!*': and the word sounded in his ears like an echo of the thought so that he realized he'd spoken it aloud while the sea still held his eyes as if it were his master or familiar that he'd addressed and now watched for an answer. Well, this was the same sea that washed the coasts of Devon, and the hours of his life that he'd spent in watching it must add to longer than he'd been now in the Azores . . .

Turning and starting down, he let the slope quicken his steps as if it drew him back towards *Revenge*; he went down the ridge north-eastwards, down inland into the valley but then north for about a mile so that he came out again upon the coast above Gadella. Then on for another mile along the very edge of the shore, following its irregular line above the rush and swirl and spouting of the foam which flung itself across the rocks and islets, battered vainly but continuously at the headlands; and when Albernas Point was no more than a hundred paces in front of him he turned right and crossed the flat shoulder of the promontory to emerge within a few yards of the landing-place and the beginning of the tents which fringed this gentler northern shoreline.

Langhorne broke silence. 'Sir Richard; the *Revenge* is being made ready for sea—'

'For *flight*?' Grenville rounded on him swiftly, and snapped the question, 'To *run*, Captain Langhorne?'

'Nay, sir!' Langhorne flushed, his usual composure broken under that icy stare. 'Prepared for sea, sir, to be ready whatever your commands. The guns run out, sir, powder—'

'Ah.' The Vice-Admiral's expression softened slightly, and he nodded. Then he turned to stare at Captain Middleton. 'So it's you, sir, who bring this intelligence that sends us scampering like rats – eh? You command the pinnace – her name escapes me—'

'*Moonshine*, sir.'

'So, *Moonshine* ... You shadowed the Spaniards from the Iberian coast, and left them near Terceira?'

'Yea, Sir Richard. As Captain Strong reported. The Dons laid off the island – Terceira – and sent in fly-boats, and no doubt learned that your squadron waited here at Flores.'

Grenville nodded. 'You kept company with their galleons several days – observed them well?'

'Ay, sir.'

Langhorne was puzzled. The information was clear enough, and quite plainly urgent. So were Lord Howard's orders. But Sir Richard asked Middleton,

'And you're in no doubt they're only twenty galleons of war, all the others merchants?'

'True, sir; but well armed, and—'

'*Twenty* men-of-war?'

Middleton nodded. 'Twenty, Sir Richard.'

Grenville's eyes found Captain Strong's, and held them. 'Yet Lord Howard intends to fly, and orders me to follow?'

Strong opened his mouth to reply, but the Vice-Admiral went on, his voice rising as his colour deepened: 'I am to *run*, from *Spain*? Lord Howard, with six fine ships of war, intends to run from only *twenty Spaniards*? When we

English are accustomed to odds of six to one and my own cousin Ralegh has written that *eight* to one should not daunt English captains?'

Langhorne saw the bulging veins at Grenville's temples; observing the signs and remembering the stories of rage beyond control, and seeing that the pinnace Captain was about to put in some words of his own, perhaps even enter into argument, he tried to catch Middleton's eye, to warn him to stay silent. Grenville shouted, 'Three years ago, how many English routed how many Spaniards in the Channel?'

Middleton said, 'Sir, I'm told your ships are short of men to sail them, let alone to fight.'

'Yea!' The word was an explosion in itself as Grenville turned and flung out his arm to point along that coastal level where tents stood in lines as shelters to the sick. 'Yea! *There*, sir – d'you see them? See them, Captain Middleton? Does his Lordship leave them here on Flores, for the Spaniards? Sick Englishmen – ay, west countrymen, what's more! – to the pleasures of the Inquisition? This is your message, gentlemen? This the command of my Lord Howard? These prime seamen of England, *since they've fallen sick they must be surrendered as easily as Lord Howard's honour*?'

Middleton could see the signs of rage plainly now, he needed no warning glance; his eyes met Grenville's and held sympathy, but if he had an answer he kept it back. Strong was more foolhardy, or less observant. He muttered, 'Sir, we'd only to convey to you the Admiral's message. To bring his order, not dispute it.'

In total silence Grenville stared at him for all of a half-minute. Then abruptly and with calculated offence, the Vice-Admiral laughed shortly, contemptuously, and turned away, and spoke to Langhorne.

'You hear that, Captain Langhorne? If I, as your commander, send you with orders to some officer of standing that he's to play the coward, d'you think to touch your forelock and run yapping to obey?'

Strong gasped, and stepped back, his hand flying to the hilt of his sword. Grenville's eyebrows rose a little, and he flicked his fingers, dismissing the gesture and immediately ignoring what had passed. Strong stood glowering, and the Vice-Admiral addressed him quietly as if nothing had happened at all between them: 'There'll be space in your long-boat for some of these men?' His eyes indicated the tents along the shoreline. 'For some who can walk?'

Strong's voice was as surly as his expression. 'My orders are to take off the chirurgeons, sir, and their mates. Even those'll more than fill the boat.'

For a moment no man spoke. Then Grenville said quietly, 'Lord Howard judges rightly that Englishmen doomed to Spanish dungeons can have no need of physic ... Ay, take 'em, then! And – Captain Middleton—'

'Sir?' Middleton's face was pale, his lips tight.

'Captain Middleton. I have a personal favour to ask of you. You may, if you wish, refuse.'

The pinnace Captain bowed slowly. 'I'm your servant, sir.'

'Thank you: be pleased to inform Lord Thomas Howard that on the squadron's return to England I shall declare his cowardice and expect to fight him.'

Middleton's eyes never left Grenville's. He nodded, but didn't speak.

'Tell him also that I shall do my duty here, and afterwards follow him to sea, as he's commanded—'

'Sir!' Langhorne was pointing seawards, towards the still anchored ships. All four of them turned to stare out across the water, and at once saw the drifting, dissolving cloud of smoke at the flagship's side even as the late sound of the gun's firing reached their ears: a second cauliflower of black smoke, and again the percussion followed: no more guns fired, but now *Defiance* had shaken loose her main-topsail, and now was clewing it again; while they watched, that sail was lowered and raised almost a dozen times; as it was clewed-up for the last time, topmen on the yard working to replace the gaskets, the flagship's standard ran fluttering up the halyards to the maintop where it flew lazily in the gentle breeze.

Grenville coughed. 'The Spaniards are in sight of your

Admiral, Captain Strong. You'd be advised to return to him without delay, for I've enough deserted men to carry . . .'

Sir Richard stood alone on the shore, watching the long-boat take Captain Langhorne back to *Revenge*, to carry out his orders, which were several.

First they were that the long-boat should return at once with as many mariners and younkers as she'd hold – and then go back for more. Drawn in close against the shore here were nine Azorian fishing-boats; strong, broad-beamed, clumsy craft which the squadron had taken from the islanders – mainly from the village of Santa Cruz – and used in the last weeks during the work of rummaging and watering. Each of those fishing-boats would need four men to handle her with those awkward, heavy sweeps the Azorians favoured; thus manned, each boat would take at least eight of the prostrate sick on the stretchers they already lay on beneath their shelters. The delay would be mostly here ashore, moving the men down into the boats, and then alongside the *Revenge*, getting them aboard.

Langhorne was to prepare the ship to receive them: tackles were to be rigged at the ship's side, for hoisting the stretchers in. (There'd be some of the sick men who could walk or crawl from their shelters to the boats; precious few with strength to climb a ladder.) More tackles to be set up for lowering the stretchers down through the hatches to the lower hold, where the men would lie atop the ballast where they'd be safe from flying shot and out of the way of those who handled the ship and served her guns. And, to an extent, their weight in the ship's bottom would assist her stability; lacking stores, she was higher in the water than she was designed to float.

Langhorne was to remain aboard *Revenge*, seeing to her readiness for sea and battle, and the spirit of her men. He was to send young Gawdy ashore in the long-boat's first return trip, to act as aide here to the Vice-Admiral . . .

'Sir Richard!'

Grenville turned: damp with exertion, pale and bright-eyed as if perhaps the fever had begun its work in his own blood, Chirurgeon Martin Willoughby, the *Revenge*'s surgeon, was trotting towards him from the tents. Scarecrow thin, and taller than most Englishmen but oddly crooked into a stoop that had become permanent perhaps from bending over his patients, perhaps from the necessity of moving about below decks during his years as a ship's surgeon, Willoughby cut a strange figure with his arms so long and hands over-large where they dangled almost at his knees: shambling to a halt as if his legs responded to his wishes only loosely, the surgeon told Grenville, 'They'll not believe me, sir. They swear they're left to Spain and – and beg me to allow them poison!' His great hands flapped like useless wings, and his deep-sunk eyes glowed in hot despair. 'As if I had poison, when my purpose is to heal!' His speech was cultured, strangely so, and his manner quite at odds with his tradesman's station. 'Sir Richard, will you speak with them? A word from you, sir—'

'Ay.' Grenville dropped a hand on his surgeon's bony shoulder as he strode past him towards the tents. This was a man he'd chosen for his own service in the *Revenge*, a man who'd sailed with him before when both of them were younger. But Sir Richard had no complaint to make of the other chirurgeons of the squadron; they'd not wanted to go with Strong, some had even questioned Lord Howard's order until Grenville had backed it with his own present authority.

The Vice-Admiral walked purposefully between the lines of tents, nodding cheerfully at the drawn, anxious faces of the sick as he passed the first ones and headed for a slightly higher place, towards the centre, from which he could address them all.

But suddenly he stopped; so suddenly that Martin Willoughby, floundering close behind, almost knocked into him before he'd first observed the halt and then induced his limbs to respond to it.

Grenville was looking down fixedly at a grey-bearded man whose fevered eyes returned his stare of recognition.

'Treganyon,' he said slowly. 'Thomas Treganyon.'

'Yea, Sir Richard.' The sick man's voice was little more than a whisper. The head and beard moved almost imperceptibly as the fellow tried to nod. 'Treganyon, sir.'

Grenville went down on one knee beside the stretcher's head. That whisper came again, strangely like sea on shingle close at hand.

'To say farewell, Sir Richard? You'll say it for me, in Kilkhampton?' Treganyon's eyes flickered up and past Grenville to glance at the tall bent figure of the surgeon who hovered like some awkward, apish spectre behind the crouched Vice-Admiral. Treganyon whispered, 'My wife's dead, sir, and the lad; but the girl's there, sir, Farmer Renlynn's wife and mother of my grandchildren—'

'You sailed with me, to Virginia.'

'Yea, sir!' The whisper rose, crusty in excitement. 'In the *Tiger*, sir, and me a Boatswain's Mate. Why, sir, there was—'

'I've passed here before, looked at you and not known you.' He spoke bitterly, seeing himself pass by, these eyes looking up and watching for recognition: he said quietly, 'Thomas Treganyon, I ask your pardon—'

The Cornishman's eyes were still on his, it seemed, but focused as if they saw through him and beyond. 'Yea, Sir Richard, I went with you into the *Santa Maria*, when we captured her on our way homeward. You remember, when we entered her, I was behind your shoulder? Sailed her here – Flores, that October, and – your orders – we hid ourselves below decks, allowing only Spaniards to be seen so they'd send out victuals from the island? Then – five men in a boat, and we held 'em as hostage and they refused us still – until that Portuguese, a passenger, knowing we'd hang 'em all if they held out against us, went ashore and coaxed 'em to give us victuals?'

The whisper broke into a chuckle, but that became a cough that racked the sick man's body and brought tears running from his closed eyes into the greyness of his beard; Grenville turned, glancing up at the surgeon, who only closed his eyes and slowly shook his head. The coughing faded, but the man's eyes stayed shut and Grenville was about to leave him when the lips moved under the tangled beard and the whisper came again but much quieter than before.

'You paid 'em for it, sir, and that I never understood, although it were in Spanish money, taken from the passengers ... But Sir Richard – you were a little boy when first I saw you, and me a lad that tended your grandfather's lawns. In the prize, the *Santa Maria*, I wanted to speak to you of that, and dared not. So now—'

'My father. You knew *him*?'

'Ay, sir. I knew Roger Grenville.'

'I was a babe when he drowned at Spithead ... But you knew him, and served my grandfather, and sailed with me – and yet, Treganyon, you believe that I, a Grenville, would leave Englishmen at Spain's mercy?'

The eyes were open, now, cloudier than before, but fixed on his. He told Treganyon, 'Listen now with care, for I must speak to all of you. While I speak, will you remember what you know of Grenvilles?'

As he rose, he turned to Willoughby. 'Give this man your greatest care. Let him go in the first boat that leaves.'

'Yea, sir.' Willoughby watched Grenville's back as he strode quickly up that incline behind the central block of tents. He saw the Vice-Admiral watching intently seawards, and the surgeon, turning, saw *Revenge*'s long-boat on its way back to the shore, crammed with men.

The sick, in their wall-less tents, mostly lay inert and listless; but eyes opened and some dragged themselves up on to their elbows as Grenville's first words boomed out above their heads.

'Hear me, Sir Richard Grenville, Vice-Admiral of this squadron and Commander of her beloved Majesty's ship *Revenge*! Now hear me!

'Ships of Spain, some of them galleons of war, are near us in the east. Lord Howard puts to sea—' Grenville paused, scowling as he hesitated over the next words ... 'And charges me, Sir Richard Grenville, to do my natural duty and then to follow him. So now you'll be carried, all of you, aboard my ship *Revenge,* and laid below, and tended by my Chirurgeon ...

'Hear me! *Revenge* shall not sail from Flores until every man, however sick, is in her!'

Cheers rose all along the shore; Sir Richard told them to rest easy, to wait their turns without impatience; he repeated that no man would be left, swearing that he himself wouldn't quit the shore until the last of them had gone aboard.

He found Willoughby still kneeling beside Treganyon's stretcher. But the surgeon's hat was in his hand; the old Cornish sailor's eyes were closed and his hard, rope-creased hands had been folded across a breast that no longer rose or fell.

The surgeon said quietly, 'He heard you, sir.'

The long-boat had landed a dozen men, and pushed off to return to the *Revenge* for more. Now some of them were hauling the first of those fishing craft to lie alongside a low shelf of shoreline convenient for the embarkation of the sick; a few others stood in a group behind John Creed, a Boatswain's Mate whom Langhorne had sent to take charge of the work on shore.

Philip Gawdy, either nervous or impatient, fidgeted at Grenville's elbow; and Willoughby, bent nearly double, stood close behind the Vice-Admiral as he gave his orders to the men.

The surgeon was to see to the well-being of the sick during their transportation; when he was sure that all was right for them at this end, perhaps half-way through the operation, he was to go aboard *Revenge* and see to their disposal in the holds. Creed and his party of younkers were to bring the stretchers down to the sea's edge and load them directly into any boat that waited for them; or, if the boats were all away, place them ready for quick loading when the craft returned for more.

Grenville nodded in dismissal; the Boatswain's Mate touched his hat and hurried up the slope with three men following and the Chirurgeon shambling ahead, making for the first tent in the line. Grenville turned to Gawdy.

'Philip, you'll remain here, if you please, and see that all goes swiftly.' He pointed inland and upwards, towards the crown of that hill he'd climbed earlier in the day. 'I shall climb up there, but remain in sight so you may signal to me in case of need. From there I may see the Spaniards, how they sail—'

His eye had noted that the other men had two boats ready and now were lounging by them, four men to each, waiting idly for the sick to be brought down. The Vice-Admiral bellowed, '*You* there! Leave two men to each boat: the rest assist your fellows!' Turning back to Gawdy, he said, 'Let none stand idle, Philip. There's little time to waste.'

Gawdy glanced seaward, then back at his Commander. 'The Spaniards are in sight of the *Defiance*, Sir Richard. Shall we have time to embark all these sick, and still escape them?'

'*Escape* them?' The Vice-Admiral's tone of voice made Philip Gawdy start, his eyes widen. '*Escape*, you say? Your choice of words offends me, Philip!'

Gawdy reddened; he was used to kinder tones than this from Grenville ... But Sir Richard's expression softened, now, and he spoke gently, carefully, as if he addressed a child.

'We do not *escape*, Philip. When these fellows are aboard, we shall put to sea—' he coughed, and paused: then continued, 'to join with Lord Howard. If the Spaniards show sense, they'll give us room enough. If they do not – well, we'll see: *and so, by God, will they!*'

Philip Gawdy nodded dumbly. He would have liked to have matched the Vice-Admiral's shout of laughter; but it wasn't in him. He looked away, towards *Revenge* again; that long-boat was on its way back with another load of men. Here, the first of the fishing-boats was already loaded, and pushing off, four men struggling with the heavy oars while there was hardly room for their feet between the stretchers with which the boat was filled. Two more of the sick were being carried down to go into the second boat.

Gawdy turned back, to find that Grenville watched him closely. 'What, you're afraid they'll catch us here? Keep us

59

from that *flota*, Philip?' He laughed again, and clapped a hand on the young man's shoulder. 'Well now, see this. From Lord Howard's maintop they'll have seen the Spaniards' topsails. Eh? And this wind's no more than light airs. Well, light . . . So there's two hours before they can be in culverin shot – and we'll be done with all this in an hour at most. Eh?'

'Ay, sir.' Gawdy was ashamed of his fear, yet not truly reassured. The long-boat was just touching shore; he looked that way, then glanced uncertainly at Grenville.

'Ay, set them moving!' Abruptly Grenville turned and moved away up the slope, striding swiftly and determinedly towards that same track he'd gone up a few bare hours ago, only then in no haste or urgency except for the urgency that had been a part of his state of mind, which had been a kind of climactic surge (as he'd known before: oh, known well, even lived with off and on over periods of years!) to that much-tasted hatred of inaction which he'd been born with and was perhaps the mainspring of his character and being: and which, those few hours ago, had turned into a mood of crystal-gazing. And now he climbed the same track and there was no longer any need for crystal, only for shrewd assessment and fast action.

Gawdy, he thought. Had I misjudged him? Was that thing I took for pure enthusiasm and which I thought could be nurtured as the eagerness (to be conditioned, but not too much, by the experience he needs) I'd want in a useful lieutenant, only a bubble of youthful naïvety which has now, in the face of danger, been pricked, and vanished? He frowned, half knowing already and for sure that he'd been wrong in thinking that he'd discovered a spirit to match his own, a man he could mould into his own outlook and, thereafter, service . . . knowing too that his own eagerness to find such a lieutenant was as much to blame as any quality or falsity in the boy.

Half-way up, he stopped and scanned as much of the sea as was visible to the east. But there was still more land than ocean, and no ship in sight. He turned, and looked back, down that slope he'd come up so fast that now his breath was short, his heart hammering; he saw boats moving in that strip of water between the shore and the *Revenge*, the ant-like figures of the men moving the sick out of their tents; they were well along the line – so the work went well . . .

One boat lay alongside *Revenge*'s waist, a stretcher hoisted in mid air as it was slung aboard; another boat was just leaving the ship's side, making way for a third that lay off, its oars spread above the water, waiting its turn to slide alongside and unload.

That went well; and beyond *Revenge*, the others of the squadron still lay at anchor.

He turned again and hurried on up the slope, steeper now, towards the summit. It would not be necessary to gain the very top, however; where this track flattened along the final ridge, from there he'd have a wide command of the island's eastern side. Not far to go . . .

Breathless, he turned again to view the squadron. *Defiance* was under way, topsails and fore-sail flattened to the wind as she beat out north-eastwards, her stern to the land. The others, too, had broken their anchors out of ground and were swinging now as their sails filled, to follow their Admiral to sea. Grenville's chest rose and fell like a bellows from the exertion of the climb as he watched the flagship gather way, her standard at the main, streamers and banners flying gaily from the fore and mizen and from the topsail yards. The course Howard had set, if he held it, would take the squadron out to clear the east coast of Corvo, but only by sailing as close to the wind as he could go. The wind was just south of east; sailing six points off it – and none of the squadron could sail closer than that without being put aback – there was the necessary margin, and no more than that, to clear the land. If the wind shifted by as much as one point, to due east, they'd be forced to put their helms up and run down on Corvo's westward side . . .

West of Corvo; glancing there, the Vice-Admiral stiffened in surprise not far from shock. Sails, that could be only Spanish – and in the north! *North!* Sir Richard strained his eyes to make them out, to tell how many . . . certainly not fifty-three. Seven – eight – ay, and a ninth astern of that – two smaller ships that might be pinnaces—

The explanation struck suddenly through initial bafflement. It was, could only be, that the Spanish Admiral, approaching from the east, had detached and sent in advance one squadron to round Corvo on the north and come down from there to block the English path downwind; that squadron which he could see (and whose topsails must have been sighted from the *Defiance* some little while ago), and the main force of the enemy, were intended to close like pincers upon a helpless English squadron still at anchor.

Swearing as he went, the Vice-Admiral hurried across the ridge to its other side; and there, spread out below him like toy ships in profusion upon a carpet of green and blue-black silk, heeling to the wind, bearing all their spreads of snowy canvas and ploughing the ocean white as they beat northwards up the island's eastern coast, sailed the grouped and ordered squadrons of Imperial Spain.

Grenville walked back downhill towards the anchorage. The urge to run – to fly! – was strong in him; but the instincts of leadership made him walk, knowing that haste on his part would breed panic or fear or at the least uncertainty in others. And besides that, he knew that the sick could not all be embarked within the space of minutes that it would take him to reach the shore if he had hurried.

That no man would be deserted, he'd given his word, openly and plainly; and even if he had not – well, there'd been no bravado in it, and that pledge, to him, was less a public promise than a part of his proper duty. The onus was in himself, to be reckoned by himself alone in terms of what was honourable and what was not; in this circumstance the same answer would have come without the slightest hesitation from his father, Roger Grenville, or from his grandfather Sir Richard, or from that earliest recorded de Grainville who came with the Norman Conqueror.

So he walked. In his mind was a picture of converging

squadrons, of courses and ships' way under varying tacks. He heard in his mind an echo of Langhorne's report: 'The guns run out, sir, powder served—' and he thought grimly but with a taste for the ingredients that was not unpleasant, 'Ay – Lord Howard's pulled the trick, he'll slip through their fingers like a greased pig. But I—!'

The role and purpose left to him was absolutely clear. First, and what was almost done, to vindicate English honour, if not Lord Howard's, by ensuring that no Englishman was left a helpless victim to the tortures of the Inquisition. Second, to show King Philip and whichever of his admirals he'd sent here with this fleet – show *every* Spaniard, and the world as well! – that an English captain would decide his own course upon the seas and hold it and see Spain damned before he'd waver from it . . .

The victuallers, and the *Ralegh*, were under way. But they were not following the squadron; clear of the headland they'd loosed all sail, and now ran north-west before the wind.

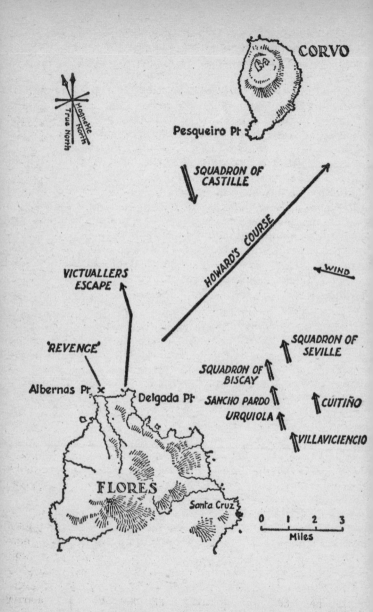

IV

'God bless you, sir!'

Faded blue eyes stared up at him from the stretcher as he halted and glanced back quickly at the man he'd just passed; a hand and arm half-raised accompanied the words, a sick man's salutation made in scant breath and strength as two younkers bent and grabbed the stretcher's ends and set off with it jogging, jolting, hurrying towards the shore.

Grenville, on his return, had appeared surprised, then dismayed, then furious to find that so many of the sick still remained on land; no one was permitted the slightest inkling that it was what he had seen from the hill that had inspired this angry, driving haste; they understood only, and all too clearly, that the Vice-Admiral had expected the work to have been much farther advanced than this by the time of his return. Only Gawdy could have asked him what he'd seen from up there, and Gawdy's inquiries had died stillborn when he'd suffered the first blast of his Commander's anger; Grenville had abused them all, but Gawdy he had singled out, accusing him of lolling and loitering and of having failed to exercise the authority vested in him by his Commander's own direct order to see that the work went swiftly in his absence. John Creed had come in for some hard words, too, and a threat of immediate demotion to common sailor; and the stretcher-bearers were bellowed at to *run*: did it matter if the sick were shaken a little, would they rather be left to rot in Spanish dungeons?

He'd no time to acknowledge that greeting from the stretcher as its carriers overhauled him, trotting shorewards. Instead, he shouted angrily to Creed, 'Is this the last?' He stared after that stretcher as if its occupant had offered him some insult, rather than a blessing.

Creed called back, 'Nay, sir – three to follow.'

That meant another boat, for those last three men, two of

whom were already on their uncomfortable, bone-shaking race to the water's edge. The man who'd addressed Grenville was at this moment being placed in the last vacant space in a boat now ready to leave; Sir Richard shouted to its four-man crew that when their stretchers had been hoisted into *Revenge* they should themselves embark, and set that boat adrift – only on *Revenge*'s port side near the stern, so that it would be out of the way of the final shuttles and carried clear by the easterly wind.

Another boat, empty, slid up to the landing-place, and at once two of Creed's helpers sprang into her while others seized the first of the last three stretchers and pushed its end across the boat's gunwale for them to take and lift; Grenville shouted, 'Boatswain's Mate!'

He'd taken no notice at all of Gawdy since he'd dressed him down, humiliating him before them all.

'Yea, sir?' Creed was in the boat, bent double, helping with the second stretcher.

'None left in the tents?'

'None, sir.'

'No doubts of that?'

The man looked up. 'Why, no, sir!'

Grenville nodded. 'Then put those last in, and then yourself and as many of your party as she'll hold. The rest may come with me in the next boat after.'

'Yea, yea!' John Creed turned, opening his mouth to give explicit orders to his men; Grenville stopped him with another shout.

'Boatswain's Mate! On your way to the ship, order one more boat to come here for me, the other crews to embark and turn their craft loose . . . One only, d'you hear?'

Revenge was ready for sea.

The sick, as they came aboard, had been put straight away into the lower holds, where the few who were still to come would soon be joining them. Martin Willoughby, the surgeon, who'd come aboard some while ago in one of the earlier boatloads, was down there with his patients in the almost total darkness (no naked flame being permitted below decks at any time) where men lay on the top of the ballast with the timbers of the deckhead only at arm's reach above their bodies; to tend them, the doctor had to crawl, and feel his way, or in places see it by the scant light that filtered down through the open hatches from the gun-decks. There was little that Willoughby could do for his charges; only, with his two assistants, chirurgeon's mates, bring water for this man to quench his thirst, spread this one's limbs more comfortably, answer groans of illness or the wildness of delirium with gruff words of comfort.

With words that could only be lies: the surgeon knew quite surely that if they were not soon landed again, or at least returned to the fresh outside air, most of these men must die.

On the quarter-deck, Pennyfeather stood with his eyes slitted against the sea's reflecting glare as he watched the diminishing shapes, stern-on, of the other vessels of the squadron. He watched, too, for the appearance of Spanish sails to the left of Delgada Point; and now and then he turned to stare impatiently shorewards, cursing in his mind what seemed to him plain lunacy in Sir Richard Grenville who was so blatantly disobeying Lord Thomas Howard's orders and, in so doing, hazarding his ship and all who sailed in her. But none of those thoughts showed in the Master's face, nor had he spoken anything of them to Captain Langhorne when a few moments ago that officer had come to discuss the general readiness of the ship.

He'd been able to inform Langhorne, however, that *Revenge* was prepared in all respects, that he needed no more than the presence on board and the instruction of her still absent Commander, to take her immediately to sea. Then he and Langhorne had exchanged a glance in which each had mentally added the words, *Before it's too late* ... And Pennyfeather, at any rate, thought angrily that it was very likely that already – too late.

But the sails were ready to be loosed and set; and the

steering was manned and tried, two quartermasters sitting down there by the whipstaff with their backs against the mizen-mast, ready to spring to their feet and take the helm as soon as the ship had way enough to feel it. And the cable had been shortened-in so that when the order came to weigh (as, please God, it would before the Spaniards bottled *Revenge* completely in this anchorage!) there'd be only a few minutes more of the capstan's heaving to break the anchor out of the sea-bed and free this galleon to her duty.

For the purpose of weighing, the boatswain (who'd seen first and personally to every other matter as the Master had ordered him) was up there now close to the fo'c'sle bitts where the cable had been stopped-up again, though only temporarily, after the ship had been hauled up to lie above her anchor, half an hour ago. Farther aft, and below decks, men lounged now against the capstan bars – four bars, three men to each bar; but here on the fo'c'sle others, including the two nippermen and the nippers themselves, who were seamen boys, sat and lay about in the galleon's bow, sprawling in the sun while they waited for the order to resume and complete the weighing. And below them, but three decks down, two men sat on the great coils of rope in the cable locker, and they also waited; it was their task to stow the cable neatly, to guide and sometimes fight it into a coil as it came down, huge and wet and heavy, all too quickly out of hand and uncontrollable if for one moment or a yard or two they let it choose its own direction and take charge of its own slithery descent.

The cable itself was too large to bend around the capstan; so to weigh anchor, it had to be dragged up through the hawse-pipe by another, smaller rope known as the 'messenger'. This had its ends spliced strongly and invisibly together so that it was in effect endless; its bight was taken around the capstan's barrel in two round turns, and a man leaning back hard on it kept weight there on those turns so that it gripped the capstan and moved with it. The anchor cable was fastened to it by short rope lashings passed in a special way by the two sailors called nippermen; they bent on their lashings, nipping cable and 'messenger' together, in

68

the ship's bow right above the hawse; then the seamen boys, known in this operation as nippers, held the lashings fast and taut and walked aft alongside the cable until, when they came to the top aperture of the navel-pipe, above the cable locker, they had to be quick in jerking the lashing clear so that the cable could slide down dripping into the dark bowels of the ship and the 'messenger' continue aft on its steady circuit of the capstan. Then the nippers would run for'ard to the bow again with their lashings, and hand them back to those two sailors who knew exactly the way to pass them around the straining, slowly-moving ropes.

Among the boys who waited on that fo'c'sle head was Jonno Wenman. He lay apart from the others, curled on his side on the deck, his torn hands clasped together between his knees. On his feet he'd seemed fit enough, agile as a nipper had to be (as indeed they all were, by this time, enjoying their own skill and deftness in holding the lashing tight until that last second when it had to be cast off from the parting ropes, neatly and quickly without a jamb or tangle and not a moment before the lashing had taken its full share of the weight for as long as it could be kept on), but now, inactive, he'd not joined in any of the talk, not even answered when his name was called; only when Wally Maine had squatted beside him, right in front of those open, staring eyes, and asked him how he felt now, Jonno had muttered in a voice so low that his friend had barely caught the words, needed in fact a moment to let them echo in his brain and there be magnified: 'I dunno what I done, Wally. What he done it to me for—'

Wally Maine had thought that Jonno had been referring to the Boatswain. He'd shrugged, and said, 'They wanted two, Jonno lad, and you was t'other. No more'n that, d'you see it? Two they wanted, and it were me and you.'

Revenge was ready for battle, too.

The guns on the upper gun-deck had been loaded with powder and shot – but not primed – and then run out, so that their grim, black muzzles protruded through those upper ports. But on the lower gun-deck where the ordnance was heavier, and the ports closer to the sea, the pieces had been charged but not run out. Those ports were still closed, because if Sir Richard intended to beat to windward as Lord Howard had done – or rather, was doing – the ship would be heeled by the wind and those lower ports could not be opened for fear of shipping water through them.

Langhorne had been in some doubt about this. It seemed likely to him that, sailing as late as this and with the enemy surely close at hand, Grenville would elect to run directly downwind, westwards, as the victuallers had done; in sheer sailing qualities *Revenge* was more than a match for any Spanish ship and a great deal faster than most, so that to take to her heels would mean almost a certainty of escape.

Well, if Sir Richard ordered such a westward course, stern on to the wind, there'd be no likelihood of heeling, and those lower ports could as well be open and the guns run out. But in such event there'd be no need of broadsides either; the ship would be running clear of Spaniards and might expect to loose a round or two from her stern-chase of demi-culverins, but no more than that.

In not running out both tiers of guns, Langhorne was risking Grenville's anger. He knew that; but it was a straight choice of actions, with good reasons for either. Logic told him that any commander would now take this vessel westward to safety, and postpone to later a reunion with the others of the squadron; and while his knowledge of Sir Richard's personality told him that logic might not play too great a part in whatever decision was arrived at, he felt too that if the Vice-Admiral's mind was set on strict obedience to Lord Howard's orders, and thus to beating out towards the east of Corvo – well, it would be at best a close thing, a race and most likely with it a running fight in which *Revenge* would need all her speed and thus every square foot of sail she had. Then beating to windward on the starboard tack, she'd heel to port; and when the ship was in that state the lower tier of guns on her starboard side could be run out, and used, for that windward side was the one that would be

engaged and the weight of the run-out guns would counter-
act the list and help to bring the full starboard broadside to
bear, which otherwise it would not . . . But one side of guns
could not be run out now, because of the list its extended
weight would give the ship . . . And – oh, it could be done
quickly enough, if the need arose. On that lower deck, although the ports were still closed, the guns had been loaded
with powder and shot, and the rope tackles overhauled and
set up taut and ready . . .

Each gun had two separate sets of tackle, one on each side
of it, for hauling it on its wooden truck carriage out towards
the ship's side until the wheels of the truck came up against
the chocks and the gun's barrel extended through the open,
square port. In action there was no need to haul it back
again; the explosion of firing flung it back all too powerfully, and those other, heavier ropes attached to ring-bolts in
the timbers of the ship's side and at their other ends, the
apex where they were joined, to the pommelion on the
breech of the gun, were called breechings and provided there
to check that vicious run-back after firing.

Cartridges had been served to the guns; first one to each,
for the initial loading, then two more to every piece. That
had made some clearance in the store, and Matthew Rolls,
the Yeoman of the powder-room, with his helpers, had
thereafter filled more cartridges with the black serpentine
powder from the kegs. The right size of cartridge, these
made of specially treated paper, was used for each calibre,
and the exact amount of powder required as the charge for
each type of ordnance then fed into it by means of measur-
ing ladles. The demi-cannon, for instance, required a
twenty-four-pound charge to fire its thirty-pound ball; a culverin only eighteen pounds to throw a lighter shot much
farther; eventually it came down to the turn of the little
falcon, needing no more than two pounds and a half.

As the cartridges were filled, the Yeoman sent a store of
them, a good number in each of the calibres, to the steward's-room, which was conveniently situated to act as a
ready-use powder store in action; it was just for'ard of the
shot-room, below the lower gun-deck's after end. That stew-

ard's-room was then shut down, its hatch locked; and having by that time prepared as many cartridges as would be needed to discharge all the round shot in the ship, the Yeoman had returned to his powder-room and made ready his supply of bombs.

These were earthenware pots which had previously been coated thickly in black pitch, and that pitch, when half dry, set liberally with leaden quarter-bullets. All Yeoman Rolls needed to do was to fill the pots with powder and then reseal them with the stoppers through which ran the fuses for ignition by the touch of a slow-match. This design was simple enough, indeed; but experience had shown that the explosions of such bombs in crowds of men, whether defenders of ships' decks or hostile boarding parties swarming over the side, could be relied upon to produce an almost incredible degree of slaughter.

Then there were the fire-pikes to be seen to: pikes just as used in close combat but with specially prepared inflammable tips and heads. These were intended for firing enemy ships which came close enough to have the pikes, already flaming, thrust into their timbers or through their ports, even down the barrels of their guns. Also in the charge of Matthew Rolls were 'arrows of wild fire', for igniting and then discharging from cross-bows into rigging or any other likely target. All these things were ready, now, implements and weapons and missiles, ready and distributed to those parts of the ship where they'd be most usefully found in battle; mostly they went into the steerage and the fo'c'sle, places under cover of overhead decks and thus protected but at the same time convenient to those who would conduct the ship's defence.

In both those compartments, too, the Master Gunner (rather, the Corporal, but acting under Joss Wenman's orders) had mounted the small quick-firing weapons known as bases. Set on swivels, the base was in fact a kind of heavy musket, only mounted; it fired six-ounce shot from multiple barrels. Breech-loading, each of the barrels was charged separately and in advance, and the pieces were mounted to fire through loop-holes in the cubbridge heads (the vertical walls

72

or bulkheads which divided steerage and fo'c'sle from the open waist deck) so as to command the waist and the whole central part of the ship. They were for use, primarily, against an enemy boarding or already on board; or, fired slantwise and outwards, to put cross-fire against him as his ship came close. At close range the base was accurate, and hit heavily enough to stop the fiercest rush.

Now ball and powder had been placed ready to these bases, of which four pointed for'ard through the cubbridge head of the aftercastle, and two aft through similar loopholes in that of the fo'c'sle. The gunners who would man them lounged in the sunshine on the waist-deck, idly, perhaps even pleasurably, watching the upperdeckmen sweat as they worked the tackles to bring the sick aboard out of the boats alongside, and then to lower those stretchers down into the holds. Other men stood near to catch sight of the faces of stricken friends and shipmates as they were swung aboard; to wish them well or give them cheer, and shudder as their prone bodies vanished slowly into the below-decks gloom and above them the sheaves of the blocks squealed intermittently their own peculiar, mournful dirge.

There were other things, too, that had been made ready.

The Carpenter, for instance, and his Mates: they'd marshalled their equipment, and prepared both below decks and above small stores from which repair action could be developed. Lead, nails, canvas, oakum, pitch; these were the materials for stopping leaks or temporarily repairing shot damage to the ship's hull; so these and the hammers and caulking irons with which they were used had been stored in key positions about the ship. In the fo'c'sle was the main store, and there too was placed rope and other gear which, in the event of the ship's sides being damaged near or below the waterline, would be used to sling one or more of the Mates over the side to repair the damage even while the galleon was still under way.

More caulking had been made ready on the lower gun-deck, in case through bad weather or heeling or battle damage it should become necessary to close and re-caulk the gun-ports on this deck or that above; and down here the Boat-swain's party had had work to do, work that should truly have been a matter for the Gunner but, by custom and to the Boatswain's customary annoyance, was established as a duty of upperdeckmen. It was the placing, here and there through-out the upper and lower gun-decks, of tubs. Their purpose was the sponging out of the ordnance; but they were not filled with salt water, which was reckoned to have harmful effects on the interiors of the gun barrels. Once the tubs were set up, the Boatswain's Mates ran through the ship inform-ing all and sundry that no man was from this moment to waste his urine elsewhere. It was needed, for the gunners' sponges.

But the Boatswain's party had other tubs to place – half hogsheads – and these, for fire-fighting, they had to fill or at any rate supply adequately with water. Buckets on ropes were flung overboard from the waist or through open gun-ports, and dragged up again to be emptied into the tubs and returned to the sea for more.

But all of this had been completed an hour ago, and a hundred other things as well; so that *Revenge*, ready now for the deep water and for the enemy, needed only her Commander.

The boat swept in and alongside and men in *Revenge*'s waist dropped ropes' ends to its bow and stern where they were caught and held; others in the boat grabbed the ship's side, using as handholds the edges of the open gun-ports, so that the boat was stopped and held against the entrance ladder formed of strong wooden battens fastened to the gal-leon's side from waterline to bulwark. Sir Richard Grenville heaved himself up, swung over, dropped lightly to the deck.

Pipes shrilled, and the lounging or working seamen and soldiers stiffened to attention. Langhorne removed his hat, and bowed; straightening, he felt his own smile of polite greeting freeze as he saw the scowl of anger on Grenville's face.

'Sir—'

'Captain Langhorne. Why is the lower gun-deck still closed tight?'

'Sir, I was uncertain—'

'*Uncertain?*' That roar of indignation might probably have been heard ashore, were any man left there alive to hear it.

'—of your intentions, sir.' Langhorne had at first been disconcerted by his Vice-Admiral's wrath; now his voice and face hardened as his own spirit reacted to the attack. He'd never taken well to bullying. He continued icily, matching Grenville's stare, '—of your intended course, sir. The guns are served and ready.'

Sir Richard held the young man's steady gaze, and there was total silence on *Revenge*'s decks as the two of them faced each other, not two paces separating them. Then Grenville nodded.

'Run out those guns, Captain Langhorne.'

'Aye aye, sir.' Langhorne replaced his hat, and turned inboard. 'Master Gunner!'

Grenville had already passed him, but paused at the foot of the ladder that led up to the half-deck. Glancing back over his shoulder, he shouted, 'Throw adrift that fish boat! Is the long-boat hoisted?'

'Yea, sir!' One of the Boatswains' Mates had answered as he hurried to the side. Arrived there, he leaned over and told the men still in the boat, 'Up with you, and cast it loose!' He stepped back quickly, touching his hat as Philip Gawdy swung his legs across the bulwark.

Gawdy was pale and silent; Langhorne caught his eye, and nodded a quick greeting, raising his eyebrows in a silent question. Gawdy shrugged, wordless and confused; his eyes moved to Joss Wenman, who'd appeared out of the hatch and now touched his hat to Langhorne.

'Sir?'

'Run out your lower ordnance, Master Gunner.'

'Aye aye, sir!' Wenman looked pleased at the order. Like a child, thought Langhorne, told he may play with all his toys at once. Well, there'd be a game of some sort, by the looks of it ... The Gunner went below like a sack of iron, covering the distance from one deck to another in a rattling crash of heels on ladder and then heavy landing; they heard his bull-bellow, 'Unstop your ports, below!' That further crash was his arrival on the lower deck: 'Run out these pieces, lads!'

On the half-deck, Pennyfeather removed and replaced his hat in one swift, practised gesture. 'To sea, sir? You'd have me weigh?'

'Ay, Master. To sea, and in Lord Howard's wake, to the eastern side of Corvo there.' Grenville pointed. 'As close to the wind as you can hold her – under fighting sails.'

The Master stood staring as if he'd been stricken senseless: as if some weight had struck him between the eyes.

'Fighting sails—'

Grenville snapped, 'Ay, none other!' Anger boiled in his eyes as he returned the Master's stare. But allowing no further discussion on that point he went on swiftly, 'Time's too short to weigh the anchor, Master. Cut the cable.'

Pennyfeather still stood there staring in what seemed to be part amazement, part horror; Grenville shouted in his face, 'What, d'you not hear me? *Cut your cable, sir!*'

The Master, his face like stone, strode aft to the break of the half-deck, and shouted, 'Boatswain, lay aft!' The word was passed for'ard, carried unnecessarily on a dozen voices, and Sturgee came running.

'Sir?'

'Have up the Carpenter with his axe, Boatswain. Prepare to cut your cable at the hawse.'

Sturgee's chin sagged in surprise. He stammered, 'Why, anchor's a-peak—'

'*You'll cut your hawse, I said!*' All the Master's pent-up anger and concern came out in that roar and with a look of such unbridled fury that the Boatswain, shocked and surprised, took a pace backwards, cannoning into a man behind him. Never before had he seen this easy-going, even-tempered seaman ruffled, let alone enraged. 'I want none of your advice, Daniel Sturgee; *d'ye hear me?*'

76

To hide his confusion, the Boatswain scowled. But he nodded. 'Aye aye.'

'Then listen.' Pennyfeather's voice dropped to its normal tones as his mind moved to the details of his trade. 'Prepare to sever the cable, to shake out your topsails and fore-sail. Well?'

'Aye aye, sir!' Touching his hat, Sturgee turned about and, pushing men out of his way, hurried for'ard, yelling for the Carpenter to make ready, for the topmen to man their yards, for the cable party to chock and secure the capstan and unship its bars, unreave the 'messenger' and double-up the stops on the cable at those fo'c'sle bitts. Its inboard end, after it was cut and the anchor let go and lost overboard, would need to be held there so that it would not all run down into the cable locker; later, there'd be the job of bending on a spare anchor, a complicated evolution requiring tackles and chains and the skilled work of the older men, the sailors ... But that would be later. For the present, as topmen raced aloft to the fore-topsail and main topsail yards, and the Carpenter came running with his axe into the eyes of the ship, there was enough to think of. Sturgee glanced aloft, and felt the wind from right ahead over the ship's bows: to turn the galleon away from the shore and to an angle where she could make use of this wind, that fore-sail would have to be braced aft on the starboard side here. There'd be orders enough flying – but that'd be the way of it ...

He pointed, and shouted to John Creed, 'Four men to the starboard fore brace!'

Philip Gawdy watched those empty, drifting fishing-boats. In the galleon's lee, they'd not gone far; they drifted slowly, singly, except for one pair which lay awkwardly locked together and turned slowly like close partners in some strange, sad dance. With the wind as it was, they'd clear Albernas Point; and there'd be nothing between them, then, and the coasts of the Americas. Nothing except 2,000 miles of sea ...

He'd heard the exchange between Grenville and the Master. Fighting sails: that meant fore-sail and topsails. Sufficient for a ship to carry way enough to move her across the sea and allow her to answer helm; but no mainsail or mizen to give her any speed, because they'd clutter the decks with gear, with running rigging, and the sails themselves might be damaged by shot and fire, and the wind in them would heel the ship and make it necessary to close the ports in the lower gun-deck. Under fighting sails alone *Revenge* could manoeuvre on an even keel, use all her ordnance and man her decks with fighting men. But under so little canvas, even a landsman could know that she'd not outsail a windward enemy. These were sails for battle, not for flight.

Gawdy, alone, shook his head. He felt an unreality in the air about him; that *Revenge* and all in her were in grave danger seemed obvious, and yet it was hard to believe that this was other than a dream, a nightmare from which he'd wake to a new day, to Grenville's friendly forenoon greeting, to a day on which perhaps the *flota*'s topsails would be spotted from a scouting English pinnace.

The *flota: that* had been the target, the enemy, the prize, the crock of gold and honour that would fall to them supported by gun-flame. Thus riches, reputation, a foot on the silver ladder of success and perhaps even a bride richer than the fortunate Bassingbourne had won . . .

Again he shook his head. The bubble had been bright indeed; and it had burst so quickly. The feeling in this ship was charged with anger, underlined with fear; he, the outsider, had been the first to feel it.

'What, pining still for Norfolk?'

Langhorne had approached so quietly, or Gawdy been so deep in thought, that the sudden voice from no more than twelve inches distance was the first sign of his presence. Gawdy jumped: and the soldier laughed.

'You seem disturbed, Philip. You'd counted over strongly on those mails from England?'

Gawdy stared at him in genuine amazement. Langhorne was in armour from the waist up to his chin, but on his head he still wore a feathered hat; the helmet, polished like the breastplate to silver brilliance, dangled on its strap from the fingers of his left hand, behind the scabbard of his sword.

'Disturbed?'

'You mean—' Langhorne waved his right hand seaward— 'You mean, Spaniards in the offing?' He nodded. 'Well, they're in force, it's true. And our Admiral's left us, that's true, too. But this *Revenge* is a fine, fast galleon, well armed—'

'We're to beat out under fighting sails!'

'Ay. More truth. From what I hear, that is.' Langhorne peered quizzically into the civilian's face, as if he found it hard to understand the reason for so much concern. 'And how else should we engage an enemy but under fighting sails?'

Gawdy stared back in angry disbelief. This was no more than pretence, play-acting. Surely they'd known each other long enough now, and at close enough quarters, to deal honestly? He said quietly, 'Sir Richard's out of his mind. We're led by a madman of some kind, he's changed—'

'Hush!' Langhorne glanced quickly round the quarter-deck. But there was no one within earshot. The nearest was Pennyfeather, who in fact was on its other side and at the top of the ladder staring for'ard over the length of the half-deck. Grenville was below, in his Great Cabin; he'd gone down there five minutes earlier, bellowing for his servant.

Langhorne allowed his mask of duty to slip a little: he told Gawdy, 'It may seem thus. Ay, so it does! But remember, Sir Richard is our Commander, and where he leads we follow. Remember too, Sir Richard has been in scrapes before. By tonight, Philip, we may all of us be cheering, and great news on its way to England.' The soldier grasped Gawdy's shoulder, and shook it. 'Now let him see your mettle, Philip! Remember how you've cried day after day for battle: now that it's come, you'd not draw back?'

'*Battle!*' Gawdy pointed eastward, at Delgada Point and the empty reach of sea where at any moment the Spaniards must appear. 'Battle – between one and fifty-three? And us short-handed! Why, that's not—'

Langhorne cut him short. He spoke almost angrily, certainly tensely, watching the younger man through narrowed eyes as if in speaking he sought to instil in him the steel of his own soldier's background: to demonstrate that private fears, or cynical detachment, which could in the long, dull days be used to foil their boredom and discomfort, had no right to exist in a moment such as this.

'By evening we'll be wherever our Commander leads us and God wills us ... We've come to prey on Spanish treasure – but there's risk in it, dangers as well as glories: if it weren't so, every Englishman alive would be here with us today!'

The soldier paused. 'How many Englishmen at Agincourt expected victory? And there's precious few of us, Philip; if honour's due, you'd not disdain a share of it?'

Philip Gawdy opened his mouth to reply; but at that moment Grenville, wearing armour similar to Langhorne's, came like a whirlwind up the ladder from the hatch and strode aft along the half-deck; his eyes blazed in his face and his lips above the beard were set in a hard, straight line. He was all vigour, purpose, powerful intent: and as he reached the ladder to the quarter-deck and flung himself up, his long sword trailing behind him, clanking as it swept the ladder's steps, Master Pennyfeather at that same ladder's top stepped aside, touching his hat, then cupped his hands to his mouth and bellowed,

'Starboard fore braces!'

The men were there already, waiting; they were hauling on that brace almost before the words had reached their ears, and the yard swung round aback to take the wind and throw the ship's bow off to port.

'Fore-topsail: let fall! Sheet home!'

On that yard the gaskets were thrown off, and the topsail fell, then tautened. Pennyfeather roared,

'Cut your cable!'

'Aye aye!' From the fo'c'sle floated back the Boatswain's acknowledgement: and in the same instant came clearly to their ears, here on the poop, the dull crash of the axe as it fell and severed the cable.

She was swinging well, off the wind now, ready for more sail, to drive her forward.

'Lee braces!'

For'ard there, the men were chanting as the topsail yards swung over.

'Main-topsail: fore-sail: let fall, sheet home!'

Revenge's fore-sail blossomed like a great white flower against the sun, and the water bubbled noisily along her sides as she gathered way towards the open sea.

V

He had only a hundred seamen to work the ship and to fight,
And he sailed away from Flores till the Spaniards came in sight,
With his huge sea-castles heaving upon the weather bow.
'Shall we fight or shall we fly?
Good Sir Richard, tell us now,
For to fight is but to die!
There'll be little of us left by the time this sun be set.'
And Sir Richard said again: 'We be all good English men.
Let us bang these dogs of Seville, the children of the devil,
For I never turned my back upon Don or devil yet.'

Tennyson
(The *Revenge*: A Ballad of the Fleet)

Captain-General Don Alonso de Bazan, Commander of the Fleet of Spain, strode briskly across the quarter-deck of his flagship, the 500-ton galleon *San Pablo*. Arriving at the port side bulwark, to which he had been drawn by a sudden exclamation from his Flag-Captain, Don Luis de San Juan, he halted, to study the extraordinary picture of a single, diminutive English galleon which apparently was so eager to play David to Goliath that it was clawing up to windward, utterly alone, out from the shelter of Delgada Point on a course that could be aimed only at interception.

Bazan half-turned his head, to put a question to Don Luis. The Captain-General's heavy brows were arched in something between surprise and amusement: yet in the profile that he presented to the other man was clearly recognizable the power and force of character of one who had in not much more than two years rebuilt and reorganized a fighting fleet for Spain. What showed in his face was more than ambition and achievement; more than the experience gained in many years of varied naval service (it was he who led the galleys against Drake in Lisbon harbour in 1587); for this Alonso was the younger brother of Don Alvaro de Bazan, Marquis of Santa Cruz and Captain-General of the Ocean Seas, veteran of Lepanto and Terceira. Santa Cruz would have led the Armada of 1588 against England; but he died in February of that year.

'That's *La Venganza* – whose commander is the Admiral Ricardo del Campo Verde, as the friar told us? You're sure?'

San Juan nodded soberly. 'It can only be ... And a madman, by the looks of it!'

Bazan chuckled; turning away from the sight of that small, distant galleon – as if perhaps he knew there'd be time enough later for a very much closer look at her – he glanced aloft at the Royal Standard that fluttered proudly from the mainmast head. It was an enormous flag of pure-white silk, bearing in its centre the Royal Arms (a shield quartered with two three-towered castles and two lions rampant, in red and gold) surmounted by a crown and encircled by the chain of the Golden Fleece.

He watched the standard, his neck bent back stiffly so that the veins stood out in protest against the tightness of his collar, for a full minute; the sight of it at his own mainmast head seemed to give him pleasure. Then abruptly he came back to earth, and told San Juan,

'Perhaps he is a little mad. From what I've heard, that could be. Yet he's a great corsair, one of the greatest of their seamen, much esteemed among them. No doubt that's why he's here: as that friar also told us, Captain, the Admiral of this English squadron is an inexperienced man, no sailor.' He shrugged. 'Of noble birth, of course.'

The friar he'd referred to was a Franciscan whom they'd questioned at Terceira, where the Spanish fleet had first touched in the Azores after the passage from Ferrol. The man had spent some days as a prisoner in *Defiance*, the English flagship, which had intercepted the small vessel in which the friar had been taking passage from Havana. His information about the English squadron had been extremely useful.

Bazan said, 'Ricardo del Campo Verde is also a great and

rich gentleman – though not exactly of the nobility. His estates and revenues are considerable; yet he's said to be a man very unquiet in his own mind – greatly affected to war.' He nodded in the general direction of the *Revenge*. 'There's proof of it, eh?'

San Juan murmured dourly, 'A bitter enemy of the true religion, sir; so the friar reported.' Piously he raised his gaunt face to survey the foremast-head, where a square banner of crimson silk carried the personal arms of Alonso de Bazan beside a crucifix at whose foot the Madonna prayed: the motto on the scroll beneath it read, *Demonstrate esse Matrem*. From that his glance swung to the main-sail, emblazoned with a scarlet cross now bellied by the wind.

The Captain-General didn't answer. He was looking again at the *Revenge* – *La Venganza* as the Spaniards called her – and watching her he smiled faintly to himself, as if indulging in some private thought that amused or touched him. Then, turning his head through some forty degrees to the right, he stared hard at the five English galleons which had been the first to come out and were now just for'ard of the *San Pablo*'s beam, still beating north-east with the wind over their starboard bows, obviously striving to cross ahead of the armada and escape the trap Bazan had set.

Don Alonso glanced aloft at the set of his flagship's sails. He told Don Luis, 'Waste not a breath of this wind. Those—' he pointed down to leeward, at Howard's ships – 'We need more of it than they do!'

He was half joking; but Don Luis only scowled.

In this squadron of Seville, which sailed as the van and spearhead of the Spanish fleet, there were two other great galleons besides the flagship. On the *San Pablo*'s port beam sailed one of her sister ships, another of the newly-built 'Twelve Apostles'; this was the *San Felipe*, commanded by Captain Claudio Beaumont. And on the other quarters was the *San Martin*; she'd been virtually rebuilt since she'd carried the Duke of Medina Sidonia as Lord-Admiral of the Armada against England in 1588, and staggered home – just – to Santander, with more men dead in her than living. Now her captain was Gaspar de Sousa; he too had served in that doomed Armada, as the senior soldier in the Grand Duke of Tuscany's galleon the *San Francesco*; and she, in the thick of the fighting from inauspicious start to miserable finish, had also got back to Spain, but in a condition that made her a total loss.

On the port quarter of the Seville squadron ploughed the Biscayans under General Don Martin Bertendona in his flagship the *San Bernabé*, another of the 'Apostles'. In the Armada of 1588 Bertendona had commanded the Levanters – from Barcelona, Venice, Genoa, and other Mediterranean ports – and he had taken a leading part in the actions off Portland Bill and Gravelines; during the latter engagement his carrack had at one point been described from another ship as having her decks in shambles, her guns silenced and blood flowing freely from her scuppers; and at that time she'd been resuming her place in the line of battle with her musketeers still ready at their stations . . .

San Bernabé was the only galleon in Bertendona's command; the other three ships were heavily-armed merchant vessels. (Like the warships, they flew the yellow-and-red striped Spanish colours, but without the small oval of a royal badge in the fly; and they wore also the Saint Andrew's cross of the House of Burgundy, but their crosses were white on a blue ground instead of red on white or yellow, as was usual for the King's ships.)

In the Biscayans' wakes sailed General Don Sancho Pardo y Ororio. His own ship was the 'Apostle' galleon *San Andrés*; he led the *Begoña de Laudecke*, the *Nuestra Señora del Pilar de Zaragoza*, the *San Juan de Carasa*, and the fly-boat *Caballero de la Mar*. Astern of them, and last in the line of leeward squadrons, came General Don Antonio Urquiola in his flagship *Nuestra Señora de Juncal*, leading four other armed auxiliaries.

The rearguard was led by General Don Bartolomé de Villaviciencio, who flew his standard in the galleon *Santo*

Thomas, which was yet another of the 'Apostles'. The others of his squadron were three galleons – the *Santiago, San Cristobal* and the *San Barnabé of Portugal* – an armed merchantman, the *Begoña-Spinola*, and the fly-boat *Leon Rojos*.

To windward – on Villaviciencio's starboard bow, and strung out abeam of Urquiola's and Sancho Pardo's ships – were General Don Luis Cuitiño's eight fly-boats, his own flag being in the *La Serena*. (Cuitiño's had been the last group of ships to join Alonso de Bazan's force at Ferrol, before they sailed for the Azores. The Earl of Cumberland, whose squadron was stationed off the Burlings, had moved fast to intercept the fly-boat squadron on its way up-coast from Lisbon: but not fast enough, since five galleys of the Portuguese coastal defence force, under Don Francisco Coloma, had placed themselves neatly between the two forces and kept Cumberland hotly engaged while Cuitiño got through to join the Captain-General.)

Away to the north-west, now beating down into the channel between the islands after rounding the northern side of Corvo, were seven galleons of Castille (and several smaller ships) under General Don Marcos de Arumburu. His flagship was the *San Cristobal*, and the powerful squadron that she led comprised the *San Felipe y Santiago, San Juan Colorado, Santiago el Mayor, San Medel y San Celedonio, San Pedro*, and the *Ascension* under Captain Don Antonio Manrique. This squadron of Castille wore their own colours as well as the royal arms of Spain: scarlet Saint Andrew's crosses blazed on fields of blue-and-white striped silk, and at the fore each ship flew the arms of Castilla y Léon.

Such was the fleet which Captain-General Don Alonso de Bazan brought to the Azores in order to overwhelm Lord Howard's puny force of English ships before the arrival of the treasure *flota* from the Indies.

It consisted in all of 33 galleons and other large, armed vessels, 8 fly-boats and 12 smaller ships, also armed; without including the fly-boats, the force mustered 722 cannon, and carried 7,500 men; of those, more than four thousand were soldiers of the Spanish and Portuguese armies.

Don Alonso stood at the for'ard rail of the *San Pablo*'s aftercastle; he stood with his feet well apart, his hands resting loosely on his silver-studded sword-belt, and looked down into the *plaza de armes* – the waist – where companies of soldiers were being mustered, their weapons inspected and ammunition issued to them for muskets and arquebuses; they were being mustered in three sections proper to their battle stations in accordance with Spanish custom – a vanguard for the fo'c'sle, rearguard abaft the mast, and the 'main-battle' in this waist-deck amidships.

The Captain-General frowned as he watched, pondering whether perhaps he'd have that section of the Fighting Instructions re-written. Drawn up in formal ranks and solid blocks, soldiers made an easy target for English marksmen: and the boarding (or rather, 'entering') intentions were always manifest to the enemy. The English were wiser, perhaps, in keeping their boarders hidden until the last moment, in providing cover, whenever possible, for the musketeers and bowmen.

Abruptly he looked up, and gazed through narrowed eyes at the English squadron; then he turned and strode aft to the higher quarter-deck. Meeting him at the ladder's top, at the carved and gilded rail, leaving the group of gentlemen with whom he'd been engaged in excited conversation about the coming battle, Don Alonso's Flag-Captain told him, 'The range is greatly closed, sir. Soon we shall have them in culverin shot.'

'Your guns are ready?'

Don Luis de San Juan nodded quickly. 'Ay, ready, sir.' He pointed at the English squadron: 'It would be wasting shot, for some minutes yet.' As he spoke he was gauging the range with his eye, perhaps actually visualizing the flight of culverin ball.

Bazan grunted non-committally as he swung round to

throw a glance at *Revenge*, now well clear of Flores. With his eyes still on her he murmured, 'Try the range in two minutes' time, San Juan. Well, say ten, perhaps ... Don't leave it too long. If our guns don't stop them, they'll be across our path and lost to me. And if *that* happens ...'

But he'd lost the train of his own words. The sentence hung unfinished in the air while his eyes stayed on *Revenge* and a smile slowly curved his full, red lips; she still held doggedly to that north-easterly course, her fighting sails trim to the wind, a pure-white stain of broken water frothing at her bow.

He muttered, 'By the Lord, this Campo Verde carries his head well up ... *gallardeando!*'

Don Luis watched too, but straight-faced, hearing the words but thinking his own thoughts, untouched by whatever feelings moved the Captain-General.

Behind them the group of gentlemen moved closer in hopes of overhearing something of Bazan's intentions.

Ignoring the Flag-Captain's silence, Don Alonso laughed aloud; then exclaimed to no one in particular, 'That *Venganza*: does she truly *sail* – or do I see her *strut*?'

Lord Howard, like Grenville, had put out under no more than fore-sail and topsails; but he had time on his side, time (with God's help) to pass ahead of the Spanish squadrons on the weather side and gain the wind in the north-east. His five galleons kept their main- and mizen-sails furled less in expectation of battle than in the intention of holding as closely as possible to the wind.

Even for Howard, it was going to be a close thing. Now on *Revenge*'s quarter-deck Sir Richard Grenville, flanked by Langhorne and Pennyfeather at his elbows, watched steadily as those squadrons ahead – Howard's dead ahead, their sterns to *Revenge*, and the Spaniards in their several powerful groups on the starboard bow – converged. Farther out on the other bow gleamed the snow-white canvas of the galleons of Castille; but that squadron was for the moment harmless, and, sailing as they had to now across and against the wind, could not bring themselves close enough to play any direct part in the immediate crisis. Only, being there downwind of Howard's present position, they made it impossible for him – had he so wished, in order to escape the Spaniards encroaching from the east – to loose his mainsails and run before the wind. Such a course would have taken him into Arumburu's arms, and those arms would surely have held him until Bazan came winging down astern.

On *Revenge*'s quarter-deck no man spoke; these three, grouped closely in its starboard for'ard corner, gazed intently over the bow to watch the slowly lessening gap between that powerful Spanish force, and the five small English galleons. From here it was impossible to tell how much lead Howard had; all that was plain was that he was holding to his course, hugging the wind, doubtless constantly trimming his sails so as to make the best use of every inch of canvas and every draught of wind, trusting to whatever lead he had and to the sailing qualities of his ships and the expertise of their Masters to outsail the Spaniards and pass ahead of them, to steal the wind. The Spaniards, on the other hand, needed to hold their position in that wind and at the same time close the distance between themselves and Howard sufficiently to bring him into the range of their guns, to damage him, slow him so that they could run down to a fight at close quarters, to grapple and board and throw their soldiers into the English ships.

But the Spaniards could not turn and run down on the English now, for all that they held the weather gauge; if they turned downwind, the English forging ahead would take the lead and the wind's advantage. This gradual closing of the range was their only hope.

Revenge ploughed gently through the dark-blue water that broke around her dipping prow and seethed and frothed along her sides, bubbled and curled and hissed under her tall, square counter where the whiteness quickly faded again so that a dozen yards astern there was no wake, no trace of her having passed. The masts creaked under wind-filled topsails, blocks rattled, rigging sang. Penny-feather's eyes roamed constantly over the sails, and now and then without turning he'd rasp an order to the Quarter-master, who'd shout the same order down to the helmsmen at the whipstaff.

'Nothing to larboard!'

'Nothing to larboard – steer fine!'

'Nothing to larboard, aye aye!'

Below, on the gun-decks, all the pieces were ready primed, their touch-holes filled with black powder from the Quarter Gunners' powder-horns. Joss Wenman had been all through both decks himself, checking each piece, seeing that lin-stocks and slow-matches were ready, tackles clear; the heavy guns – demi-cannon and cannon-periers – had, on Gren-ville's orders, been loaded with cross-bar shot, ready to give any enemy that came to sufficiently close quarters the most devastating broadside that could ever be dispatched. But if there was to be a fight – and it was impossible to think, now, that one could be avoided – it would be the culverins that would have first chance to speak. They had greater range than any Spanish gun; at least, that had been so in recent years, and was well proved three years ago against the Armada. To hold your distance and hit the enemy at a range where his own guns were of little use; these tactics had car-ried many an English ship and squadron to victory. But to hold your distance, you needed the advantage of the wind; and the Spaniards sought that same advantage for exactly the opposite purpose, to run down and grapple ship to ship, hand to hand.

Along the sides of *Revenge*'s waist, 'fights' had now been rigged. These were screens of coloured cloth set up on lines above the bulwarks so as to raise their effective height and thus hide, from an enemy, the movements of men about that deck. For much the same purpose, and again on Grenville's orders, heavy rope cable had been coiled down in suitable places on the waist, half-deck and fo'c'sle to form protective nests in which musketeers or pikemen could crouch to await the onrush of enemy boarding parties, the walls of thick rope around them serving as protection from the bullets of

Spanish marksmen in the high castles and rigging of the attackers.

And the drums were beating now to quarters, sending all hands scurrying to their action stations above decks and below.

Philip Gawdy was very conscious of the weight and shine of his armour's breastplate. He'd equipped himself in London, on the eve of *Revenge*'s departure for Plymouth to join the others of the squadron, and written that night to his brother Bassingbourne describing his accoutrements as being 'the very fellows to my Lord Thomas and Sir Richard'; yet, dressed now in all martial glory, he felt himself to be more an actor, a performer, than a man of action. Now he climbed the port-side ladder to the quarter-deck and crossed over to its starboard side to stand diffidently behind the others. Grenville glanced quickly over his shoulder; surprisingly, he turned, and smiled.

'You've waited for this day, Philip. Eh?'

That smile, containing all the old warmth, was infectious; it took Gawdy back to a dozen or more occasions when, basking in the evident approval of his Vice-Admiral and bubbling with eagerness for a fight that would be all victory even before it began, he'd stood like this, and chatted, and exulted, revelling in his own good fortune. Now he smiled back, forgetting for a moment the bitterness, the doubts, that fear which shamed him but remained . . .

'Ay, Sir Richard.' Hardly conscious of his own words, he asked, 'Shall we be at them soon?'

Grenville threw back his head, and laughed. Langhorne chuckled, his eyes warm with a mixture of surprise and approval. Pennyfeather frowned, glancing in something like disgust from one face to another and at the same time moving slightly away from the three of them as if he needed to place physical distance between himself and this small circle of insanity.

Grenville shouted, '*At* them? Ay, *at them*! What, Master, d'you hear that?' Still laughing, he'd turned, but seeing the Master's gloomy, morose detachment his own smile vanished and for a moment the two stared at each other in silence. Then Sir Richard snapped, 'Fetch me your boatswain, Master Pennyfeather.'

Pennyfeather nodded; turning, he shouted for'ard, 'Boatswain! Boatswain Sturgee, lay aft!'

Daniel Sturgee came running along the half-deck; in a few seconds he was at the top of the ladder, and Pennyfeather told him curtly, 'The Commander.' Sturgee touched his hat to Grenville. 'Yea, sir?'

'Out with your flags and streamers, Boatswain. Ay, and send me here my trumpeter and drummers. Yarely, d'you hear?'

Streamers, from the tips of the yards, of red and blue and gold; the ship's own ensign on her quarter-staff; banners at foremast-head and mizen, these also in blue and red but bearing the Royal Arms and Her Majesty's badges in silver and gold; then falcons, lions ... When the ship was fully dressed, displaying her colours and with them her loyalties, and above all – at the main – the cross of Saint George, Grenville glanced about her masts and yards, and nodded in satisfaction. Smiling, he told Gawdy, 'Now, by God, they'll *know* us, when we're at them!'

Langhorne murmured, 'Drummers, sir, and the trumpeter.' The three men with their instruments were grouped at the ladder's foot, waiting for orders.

Grenville jerked his head. 'Stay them on the half-deck.' He laughed, and told Gawdy, 'When the time's fit, we'll give the Dons a tune; we'll see them dance! Well, Master?'

Pennyfeather had turned as if in sudden decision, or – by the look on his face – exasperation. He'd taken two or three steps towards Grenville and now faced him squarely, stolidly.

'Sir Richard, with respect, but as Master of this galleon, I say we should cut loose the mainsail.'

Blood suffused the Vice-Admiral's face. '*You* say: you *dare* to say—!'

'Ay, sir.' The Master half turned away to point at the Spaniards on that weather bow. 'It's my duty, sir, to speak out . . . *That* way, Sir Richard, is madness. But if we should bear away, *now*, no later—' Swivelling again, his body moving with the slow deliberation that marked the delivery of the words themselves, he pointed out over the port bow where the squadron of Castille was still beating in from the north-north-west, 'and run west under full sail, we'll be across the bows of that squadron, and fall clear, and save this ship, sir, for Her Majesty; ay, and our own lives too, and those poor wretches down below—'

'Enough! *Enough*, by God!'

Grenville's face was twisted in rage and his eyes bulged as he stared in utter loathing at the man who'd dared to suggest that he should turn and run from the enemy. But when after a short space of shocked silence he spoke again, it was in a lower, carefully restrained tone; he'd taken control of that fury, or masked it, only the sudden pallor of his cheeks told of the emotion riding in him.

'Master Pennyfeather. I thank you for the advice you offer – with such freedom. But my course is set and shan't be changed . . . Now hear this – and you, gentlemen!' For a moment his eyes shifted to scan the faces of the other two. Looking back at the Master, he continued, speaking quietly still yet almost spitting each word into Pennyfeather's expressionless eyes, *'I would choose rather to die, than to dishonour myself, my country, and this Her Majesty's ship, by turning from the enemy.* Why, death . . .'

Instead of finishing that sentence, he stopped abruptly and turned away; Langhorne, behind him now, saw that the Vice-Admiral's hands, the one hanging loosely at his right side and the other resting on the hilt of his sword, were shaking violently.

'Master Pennyfeather: I'd have you know my full intentions.' Grenville's right hand was raised now, pointing at the nearer of the Spanish squadrons on that weather bow: the squadron of Biscay: then, swinging round, over the other bow at the oncoming galleons of Castille.

'I'll pass between those squadrons, holding this course in

Lord Howard's track; and that done, being passed through them and using my guns as may be necessary, '*I'll force that squadron of Seville to give me way* . . . D'ye hear me?'

Now he'd whirled again to face them, his eyes swiftly examining them for their reactions. Gawdy, unable to judge or assess the situation and still fearful, but remembering the soldier's advice and the even more recent encouragement of Grenville's renewed approval, nodded dutifully. Langhorne nodded too, and spoke his acceptance.

'Yea, Sir Richard.'

Grenville turned back to the Master. His voice rose high, and his expression was as plainly menacing as the words:

'Hear this now, Master. If any man lays hand upon that mainsail, or orders another man to do so – *then, by God, I'll hang him from its yard*!'

There was no possible doubt that he meant exactly what he said. Langhorne stiffened: Gawdy caught his breath. Grenville demanded quietly of the Master, 'D'you hear me?'

Pennyfeather's face was rock. 'Yea yea, Sir Richard.' He allowed Grenville the suggestion of a bow; then turned to move away but paused again, his eyes resting on the soldier in something between surprise and disappointment. Langhorne returned his glance for a moment; then, apparently embarrassed, looked away, out over the starboard bow where Howard's five galleons showed their sterns and top-sails in a small, tight group.

'Sir Richard!' Langhorne was pointing: Gawdy and Pennyfeather whirled about. But Grenville, having to his own satisfaction disposed of the Master's opposition, had been looking that way too, and he'd seen – as Langhorne had – the smoke of gun-fire spurt from the squadron's star-board side and drift back quickly on the wind, momentarily to shroud from here the view of the ships themselves. Now came the sound of that broadside, a harsh rumble that reached their ears at the same moment as the squadron of Seville fired an answering broadside; it seemed far heavier, a whole wall of smoke that drifted slowly across the surface of the sea towards the English ships.

94

Gawdy realized that he was witnessing his first fleet action at sea. He moved a little to one side, beyond the Master, so as to have a clearer view.

Langhorne muttered, 'I've seen no shot hit, sir, nor fall.'

'Nor I.' The English had fired again: or other of the ships had done so. At that range they'd be using only culverins, and there'd not have been sufficient time for reloading in that short interval.

Grenville observed, calmly, 'Lord Howard's slipping past them.'

Langhorne nodded. 'Ay. If he's not badly damaged by their guns. And he's unrigged; the Dons have less to shoot at than his gunners have.'

But Sir Richard had not been making conversation; his remark had been only the spoken beginning of a train of thought. Now he barely heard Langhorne's words while his own echoed in his mind and to himself he added, Then soon, if they fail to cripple him, he'll be by them, and in possession of the wind. Will he *use* it? With his five ships, he could hold to windward of the Seville squadron and keep them lively with his culverins and come to little harm himself: if he does that, then we in *Revenge* may find our road more clear!

The Spanish squadrons had the look of cities of tall, white houses afloat upon the pastures of the sea. Downwind, the English force, by the same viewpoint in imagination made a tiny village of low, white cottages. Well, size meant little, for the English ships were speedier and more weatherly and certainly for their size no less well armed. When the Spaniards fired – as they did again, now – the smoke of the discharge rolled down towards the English in a heavy, solid cloud of black and grey; when the English answered – and there, that was an English broadside! – the smoke was a puff that swirled and vanished almost at once. But the direction of the wind had a deal to do with that . . .

Grenville turned to Langhorne. 'That Spanish broadside was only from their leading galleon. Did you note that? And – oh, see there! D'you see? Only their van fired! By God, Howard's past them!'

'Ay, sir.' As the soldier nodded agreement, they saw another English broadside, and the smoke of it, hardly visible for there was so little, showed without doubt that only the rearmost ship had fired.

So Lord Howard had, indeed, passed clear of the Spanish advance; now he had the wind, or at any rate was in a position to take it. Another thought struck Grenville: that if the Spanish Commander decided now to contend the wind, to bear down and trim his sails so as to steer a course parallel to Howard's, then he'd be moving his ships out of *Revenge*'s path. Even if he took *one* of the squadrons . . .

Pennyfeather turned his head a fraction. 'The Dons are changing course, Sir Richard.'

A smile lit Grenville's face. The Master was right: those distant shapes were changing slowly as the great galleons of Spain swung ponderously to a new course.

Gawdy strained his eyes to make out what was happening, out there on that expanse of ocean where battle seemed as slow-moving and impersonal as the march of clouds across a listless summer sky. All he saw were shapes, ships, sails; they told him no story, gave him no answers as it seemed they did to these others' eyes. The picture he looked at was remote, a painting that moved, the movement itself so slow and small as to be imperceptible: motion was evident only because the picture looked different now from its appearance half an hour ago . . . Guns had been fired, but that too was a fact without meaning or at any rate immediacy, a fact and nothing more; men may have died, but if they had their suffering was so far removed from reality by the intervention of those few thousand yards of sea that the thought of it was less vivid than an account of the same affair would have been, in some London gathering, six months after the event.

Gawdy was at first annoyed and then appalled by his own sense of detachment; he tried to force himself to feel, to be moved in some way by what he'd seen and heard and knew to have been happening; but he could not, and it angered him.

The Master spoke again to Grenville.

'They've borne up. Turning to larboard: ay, and dousing topsails.' His tone was ominous. Now he turned his head. 'D'you see that, Sir Richard?'

Grenville didn't answer, or even show he'd heard. But he'd seen it: against his will and prayer he'd recognized, in the last few seconds, that the Spaniards had altered course to port and not to starboard as he'd hoped they might.

They were letting Howard and his squadron go: turning downwind and shortening sail so as to drop down in crushing force upon this single galleon.

VI

Thousands of their soldiers look'd down from their decks and laugh'd,
Thousands of their seamen made mock at the mad little craft
Running on and on, till delay'd
By their mountain-like San Philip that, of fifteen hundred tons,
And up-shadowing high above us with her yawning tiers of guns,
Took the breath from our sails, and we stay'd.

Tennyson
(The *Revenge*: A Ballad of the Fleet)

'*Now be ready!*'

Two men roared it, their shouts so close together that they came almost in unison; the order had come first from the Master Gunner, Joss Wenman, who'd taken up his position in the hatchway that led down from the steerage compartment to the upper gun-deck; on this ladder, up and down it, he was close enough to take directions from Langhorne or Grenville above him on the upper deck, and from the top of it look out through the steerage ports to have his own clear view of the enemy and the fall of shot; and also he was there in sight and sound of the gun-decks, in touch with his Gunner's Mates – Rowan and Hardcastle – who had charge of the two decks of ordnance. It was Will Hardcastle, here on the upper gun-deck, and Alec Rowan down below, who'd just yelled that stand-by order to the captains of the guns.

Each gun captain had already primed his piece, first pushing a priming-iron down through the touch-hole both to clear it and to prick a hole in the paper binding of the cartridge, then filling the touch-hole with powder from his horn. Now at the shouted warning each one fitted a glowing slow-match into the fork of his linstock and stood tensely beside his gun, ready to put flame to powder. The guns' crews stood aside, too, close against the ship's hull between the guns, well clear of the paths of their violent recoil.

Wenman bellowed, 'Starboard culverins and demi-culverins alone! All others hold your fire!'

The Mates passed on the order to their decks, although Joss Wenman's bull-roar had been clearly audible to every gunner: must indeed have been heard by those sick men down below in the darkness of the holds.

(Those sick were on their own, now. Chirurgeon Willoughby had set up his headquarters in the Great Cabin, preparing there his instruments – knives and saws and clamps, medicaments, needles and balls of thread – and laying out on the great oak chest a sailcloth pallet which transformed it into an operating table. As usual on these occasions, he was hampered by being allowed no fire for preparing pitch or heating water. No flame was permitted below decks, now that powder had been served to the guns and to the ready-use store; the fires in the brick-floored cook-room, which occupied a for'ard section of what was properly the lower gun-deck, had been doused some hours ago.)

Now on that lower gun-deck the captains of the midship demi-cannon stood back, bringing their linstocks well clear of the breech-ends of their pieces where they'd been holding them in readiness for the order to give fire; on the upper gun-deck the cannon-perier and saker gunners similarly relaxed. Up here, in fact, only one gun captain still made ready, for except for the one pair of them just abaft the capstan's barrel all the demi-culverins were in the bow- and stern-chase. The guns' crews, having no immediate duties, clustered between the long, black shapes of their pieces, peered out around the edges of the open ports to watch the enemy approach. *Revenge* pitched gently as she forged slowly through the sea which hissed and bubbled on the other side of those stout timbers; as she pitched, her masts creaked rhythmically, and from above came the sounds of straining cordage, orders and acknowledgements as the Boatswain kept the sails trimmed precisely to the wind ...

Wenman roared, 'Starboard culverins – *give fire!*'

The slow-matches dipped, crimson arcs of light in the gloom of those low and narrow decks; at the touch-holes of the culverins, powder spluttered and spat.

Philip Gawdy held his breath, waiting for the thunder of the guns beneath his feet: he waited for that, and at the same time watched spellbound as that seemingly vast galleon on the starboard hand bore down upon them, a mountain of timber and canvas and jutting guns, a citadel of armoured men whose wild laughter and shouted taunts had come – and still came – in offensive answer to the fanfare and the roll of drums from *Revenge*'s quarter-deck.

Abuse and contemptuous merriment came from all those Spanish ships; but none of them, yet, had fired a shot. Now this great one – there were others as big, but none bigger – was dropping down ahead and out of the Spanish formation, plainly intending to board and grapple. She was three times the size of *Revenge,* and her wide decks were thick with soldiers . . .

The broadside crashed out from *Revenge*'s starboard side: the stinging reek of powder struck him, filling his eyes and nostrils as it was flung back on the wind: his ears sang with the noise of the cannon as he gripped the top of the half-deck bulwark and watched the Spaniard, saw timber splinters flying as the balls struck home, saw a group of soldiers beside her mainmast flung apart, one smashed body hurled, contorted, against the cubbridge head: an open mouth, screaming, an arm—

'*Sakers give fire!*'Langhorne barked the order from the quarter-deck; below him, the quartermasters at the whip-staff echoed the words, and Joss Wenman's bellow boomed out below decks.

'*Larboard culverins: give fire as you bear!*'

Gawdy, half dazed, looked out to the galleon's other side, the lee, where the squadron of Castille had hauled them-selves just barely into range. Those seven galleons had ex-changed long-distance shots with Howard, on opposite

100

courses, before he'd left them beating vainly against the wind; since then they'd closed the range and now gone about on to the starboard tack to sail parallel to *Revenge*'s course. Being ahead of her, although downwind, they'd now brought themselves close enough to threaten her as she came up abeam; so Grenville had not only to fight off the starboard squadrons if he was to win past them to follow in Lord Howard's track; he'd also to fend off the pincer's other claw.

The deck quivered under Gawdy's feet as the four starboard sakers discharged their shot and flame: immediately after came a single deafening crash as the saker in the Great Cabin, only a few feet from where he stood, added its lonely contribution: then the port-side culverins began to fire, one piece at a time as the leading Castillian swam into the gunners' sights.

He looked back to starboard, at that great galleon bearing slowly down upon them. Her decks were in disorder, now, the ranks and knots of soldiers broken and disrupted by the sakers' six-pound balls, aimed high with that precise intention. But still she looked closer every moment: and now, from the whole of her length, fire and smoke belched from three tiers of cannon.

A sledge-hammer, to swat a fly . . .

Gawdy's body wanted to fling itself prostrate on the deck, behind the shelter of this bulwark. Bent double – though not consciously having bent or even moved – he turned and looked frantically towards the poop, to see how the others took cover, or where, to know for himself what protection he might seek . . . He saw Langhorne coming towards him, rattling down the ladder to this half-deck, calling over his shoulder to Grenville who stood quite erect at its top. Perhaps, thought Gawdy wildly, they hadn't seen or heard the Spaniard fire? Sir Richard evidently had given the soldier some order; as Langhorne came for'ard, moving briskly but not, it seemed, in haste, Grenville turned from him and stared out towards the enemy; at that moment, as Gawdy noted in amazement the calm, almost pleasurable expression in the Vice-Admiral's face, in that split second in which he'd seen the enemy fire and bent and turned and seen

101

then – but only as a distorted, incredible picture remembered from blurred glimpses of nightmare – the bizarre insouciance of both Grenville and Langhorne, the Spanish broadside struck.

A chunk of the mizen-mast the size of a large cheese broke away in a shower of small splinters and fragments of wood which vanished as quickly as a puff of smoke; Gawdy saw Grenville turn and inspect the gouge in the mast with something of aloof annoyance in his manner, as if perhaps the mast was to blame for giving way so easily to Spanish metal: at the same moment there was a howling, rushing sound overhead and, simultaneously from somewhere below decks, a noise of shattering timber and a moment of dead silence before sudden, terrifying screams of human agony.

Langhorne clapped a hand on Gawdy's shoulder. 'Sir Richard calls you, Philip!'

He had to shout above the noise of *Revenge*'s guns, but there was no alarm or urgency in his voice; it could have been raised only to pass some message above the noise of wind, or storm. Gawdy stared at him blankly, hearing the words but barely understanding them: Langhorne jerked that shoulder, turning him, gave him a push in the direction of the quarter-deck.

'The Commander, Philip! *Quickly!*'

Langhorne dropped down on to a step of the ladder beside Joss Wenman, and grasped the Master Gunner's arm. It was as thick and hard as the loom of a long-boat's oar.

'Your lads do well, Gunner!'

'Ay, sir.' The man frowned. 'Yet—'

'Now hear this. Your higher tier to continue shooting as fast as they can be loaded and still bear. Likewise the smaller guns above. But the lower deck and the periers, with them hold your fire until I pass the word. Ay, and the portpieces aft there—' Langhorne jerked his head towards the Great Cabin— 'Those too, wait for my command ... Well?'

'Yea yea!' Wenman turned, shouting instructions to his

102

two messengers – seamen boys, the same age as his son. He sent them scampering, carrying his orders to the falcon gunners in the fo'c'sle and aft to the battery of sakers and port-pieces in the Great Cabin. He yelled after them, 'Jump to it, lads! *Fly!*'

Then, climbing down to stand in the gun-deck itself, he yelled his orders to the quarter gunners and gun captains, and Langhorne heard Rowan, on the deck below, take up and repeat the orders as they affected his own batteries. Wenman climbed back on to the ladder, and placing his mouth close to Langhorne's ear he shouted above the noise of firing, 'One of my own Mates killed, sir – Will Hardcastle. Him and two o' that for'ard saker's crew. Chain-shot it was, largely through that port—'

'Hardcastle . . . Two others. So early—' Langhorne peered for'ard through the noisy, crowded, half-lit gun-deck. Nothing up there was visible: only the shapes and silhouettes of bent, moving men, guns firing, recoiling, eddies of smoke, the pungent acridity of powder fumes, guns being dragged back loaded to their ports . . . He asked Wenman, 'None other hurt?'

'Ay, sir, Splinters. They fight on. But Hardcastle: and Carew, and young Thomas Meade—'

Chain-shot: that was in the demi-cannon and the periers, too; soon the Spaniards would have a taste of it. But for now those larger guns were silent, their crews impatient, scowling, burning to throw their own metal into the fight, disliking and not understanding the order to hold their fire when the Spaniards were already quite plainly in range of every gun in the ship. But even the culverins had fallen silent, now, in obedience to Langhorne's orders. The gunners' eyes gleamed white in their already powder-blackened faces as on both sides of the ship they crouched beside their guns and stared out from gloom to brilliant light to watch that ever-shortening range.

'Then – that saker's crew?'

'I've moved men from other pieces, sir.'

Langhorne nodded. 'The hull's not damaged?'

'Yea, sir. Timber's cracked about that port.'

In front of them the starboard demi-culverin fired, all noise and flash and flying sparks and the cloud of dense black powder-smoke and the vicious backward rush of the gun itself, then the hard cracking thud of the breeching ropes flying taut to check that rush, stopping the gun dead so that the impetus and the sudden brake of the heavy ropes flung the gun and the truck it rested in several inches clear of the deck; it crashed down again and was still smoking and its crew were at it at once. First the worm, a kind of cork-screw on a pole, was pushed down from the muzzle through the whole length of the gun, and then jerked out again, bringing with it fragments of smouldering cartridge-paper; then the sponge went in, a sponge also lashed to a pole, and soaked in urine; then the gun captain, who meanwhile had reamed the touch-hole and blown through it to make sure no glowing specks of powder still remained, fed into the muzzle the paper cartridge that held twelve pounds of black serpentine powder. He slid the cartridge in from its ladle, and after it the wad and the ten-pound ball, four inches in diameter; a man beside him placed the rammer in his hands, and he used it deftly, expertly, ramming home charge and wad and shot not too lightly, not too hard, and stepped aside, whipping the rammer out with his left hand in one swift flowing movement, the shaft of it running on through the loose circle of his fingers until its head came up against them; stepping back, he flipped his right hand as a signal to the others who had by now manned the tackles and at once flung their weight on the ropes to haul the ten-foot-long weapon back into its firing position in the gun-port while he himself poured powder into the touch-hole. Then the gun captain stooped, peered along the line of the barrel against the brilliance of the day outside *Revenge*'s jolting, shudder-ing hull: nodding to himself, he straightened, stepped back a pace, glanced behind him to see that the path of recoil was clear: and again, that glowing slow-match dipped towards the touch-hole . . .

*   *   *

'Then, Master, you'll be ready?'

'Yea, sir. Though—'

'*What?*'

Pennyfeather, in his heavy leather jerkin, a protective jacket no different from that worn by any seaman or soldier whose action duties brought him to the upper deck in reach of arrows and musket balls, looked underdressed as he faced Grenville in armoured breastplate.

'Ay, Sir Richard. I'll be ready.' He paused, as if he had more to say but doubted the wisdom of continuing: and decided not to. Instead, he nodded again. 'Yea, sir.'

Gawdy, at Grenville's side, had heard the plan. The heavier guns were to be held ready until the Spaniard was at point-blank range; then the starboard broadside would be given her in one great hammer-blow, and *Revenge* would be put about, turned on her heel towards the enemy, giving him the fire of the bow-chase as she turned, and on round to the port tack to gather way again and cross his stern and in so doing to deliver the same smash of heavy shot from her port batteries; crossing that Spaniard's stern then, she'd be between them all, among them, her starboard guns by that time reloaded and all the higher ones in action all the time, firing as fast as they could reload and find targets on her beams; using, too, bow- and stern-chases whenever they came to bear on Spanish hulls. From that point, taking the Dons by surprise in the quickness of her change of course, she'd find her own way through them, trusting to her own weatherly qualities and comparative ease of handling, being so much a smaller ship than any of the Spaniards, needing less wind to move her, presenting so small a target and so low in the water, too, for their higher rows of guns ... Perhaps, if all went as it might, she could be thrown back on the starboard tack once she was inside their lines, and fight her way through between them while they'd be hampered in their shooting for fear of hitting each other ... Perhaps, though, beat on to windward, staying on the port tack and passing mainly astern of the Spanish squadrons to gain the wind from them before they could throw themselves about.

Once with that advantage of the wind, if it could be won, *Revenge*'s sailing qualities would do the rest.

Grenville's eyes gleamed with excitement as he watched the lessening distance between himself and the Spaniard. He said, half to himself and half to Philip Gawdy, 'To win through *there*: to take that wind and beat up: ay, to have been among so many and given them a taste of shot in their bellies, spilled a little blood and then *adieu*!' He chuckled between his teeth and almost shouted, 'Ah, a royal thing, by God! *A royal thing!*' His eyes gleamed, and he thought, A chance such as Francis Drake would give his own right arm for!

Gawdy asked him diffidently, 'Why do they hold their fire? After that one broadside—'

Grenville's face darkened. 'They presume to take us, boy, not sink us. Since this war began they've not taken one English ship, not one; while tens of theirs have struck their colours to smaller English squadrons.' Scowling, the Vice-Admiral pointed at the enemy ships. 'See how their decks are filled with soldiers? They seek to grapple to us, board and enter, fight a land battle on our decks, smother us by weight of numbers. They see us alone, unsupported against all their fleet, and dream of bringing us into Lisbon under Spanish colours.'

He turned his head and spat high to leeward, giving it to the wind. He told Gawdy, '*There*'s your reason why the devils hold their fire!'

(The Spaniards would get more than chain-shot when *Revenge* passed by and through them. At Grenville's orders the Corporal had stationed crossbowmen out of sight in the fo'c'sle and in the Master's cabin, the round-house right aft on this quarter-deck: they had arrows of fire, to be ignited and then shot into enemy sails and rigging, and a good supply of bombs for hurling down into crowded Spanish decks as *Revenge* swept by.)

Now to windward there was nothing to see but Spanish ships, high-castled, bristling with men and guns, great clouds of wind-filled sails emblazoned with the hated emblems and colours of Philip's Spain. Small-arms could reach them now,

106

and the Corporal had muskets and arquebus men busy at the fo'c's'le and Great Cabin ports, firing as they could when the guns there were back for reloading. Others took aim from the shelter of the bulwarks in the waist where they were screened, too, by the cloth fights strung on lines along both bulwark-tops.

Langhorne's head and shoulders appeared above the ladder from the half-deck; in a moment he was with the others on the quarter-deck, and saluting Grenville.

'The gunners have their orders, sir.'

Grenville nodded. Langhorne told him, 'There were three men killed from that Spanish broadside. One of the Gunner's Mates, Hardcastle, and two of a saker's crew.'

Again Grenville nodded, but distantly as if he'd barely heard.

'Master!'

'Sir?' Pennyfeather came closer, peering stolidly at Grenville under the rim of his steel helmet. 'Yea, sir?'

'The mariners are ready for your orders to put the ship about?'

The Master allowed himself a slight frown, as if the question puzzled him. 'Why – yea, sir!' He glanced for'ard, as if he might see there some explanation for whatever doubt was in the Vice-Admiral's mind. 'All's ready, sir—'

'I'll have no delays, Master, no slowness. Shan't you warn them, for'ard there, of my intention?'

Pennyfeather's face cleared: so *that* was it. But he shook his head firmly. 'Nay. If I warn my Boatswain, however I may tell him now stand fast, he's bound to put men handy to the braces. Then if the Don has his wits with him, and sees that, likely he'll be ready for our change of course.' Pennyfeather's eyes were fixed steadily on Sir Richard's. He added, 'They know their duty and should do it without warnings, sir – if I may say so.'

'You may.' Grenville nodded, his expression almost friendly – perhaps because he recognized that the man had been talking sense.

'But, sir—'

Grenville looked at him sharply, suspiciously.

'Well?'

'If I may say this, sir – and speaking as a seaman and this galleon's Master – then sir, I'd say you'd be ill-advised to close the range too finely before you put the ship about. There's little water there between us; and if we fall into his lee—'

'Ay, Master. Thank you.'

Grenville's tone was curt again, his words more a rebuff than acknowledgement. He turned his back on the Master, dismissing him; plainly that earlier dispute still rankled. Langhorne, watching both men unobtrusively, realized that if they came through this action alive and afloat, Penny-feather would not be likely to escape the consequences of his recent errors of judgement. Most likely Sir Richard would not wait to be back in England to lay charges; he'd call a summary Court Martial, here at sea aboard *Revenge*, probably before he even rejoined the others of the squadron. The charge: advising and entreating his Commander to turn and run from the face of the enemy, to the detriment of Her Majesty's honour, etcetera ... Langhorne thanked his own good sense for the fact that although he'd had his private doubts and hesitations, he'd kept them to himself and not backed the opinions of the Master.

For now there was indeed a chance: if the manoeuvre were executed smartly, taking the enemy completely by surprise, there was a *good* chance that Grenville might turn the tables on the Spanish Commander; and what was more, the move was justified entirely if one considered the Fighting Instructions penned by Grenville's own cousin, the illustrious Ralegh. There was in them a general but specific order 'to batter them in pieces, *or force them to bear up and so entangle them, and drive them foul of one another to their utter confusion*'.

If *Revenge* went about now as Grenville planned, forced a path between the rearmost of the enemy and took the advantage of the wind, she'd be doing exactly that – as well as saving herself and giving Spain a lesson that would shame her seamen for a hundred years to come!

Yet, thought Langhorne tensely, biting his lip and feeling

108

the sweat damp within his armour, Master Pennyfeather was absolutely right in what he'd said. Grenville should listen to him, take note of advice born of a lifetime's experience on the sea: if it were not that they'd already quarrelled, and on an issue of such gravity, there was little doubt that Grenville *would* have listened. And, at about this moment, be putting *Revenge* about, flinging her round on to the other tack in a thunder of guns and cheers.

The plan was good: only the timing—

Pennyfeather shouted suddenly, '*Now*, Sir Richard! Else it's too late!' He was pointing over the side, at the surface of the sea ahead and on their starboard bow. Spinning round, he asked Grenville urgently, 'Go about, sir?'

Grenville was already moving to the ship's side, his face hard with anger. 'What, Master? *What?* Why, damn you if—'

'Look there, sir! In no time ye'll be in her lee, and stayed, by damn! Then she'll *have* us!'

For two or three seconds that seemed to Langhorne like an hour of static time, Grenville stared at that expanse of glassy, unruffled water into which *Revenge* was heading. Then he turned inboard, and glanced aloft at the topsails. They still held wind.

His eyes came down to meet Pennyfeather's.

'Ay, Master. Put her about.'

Pennyfeather whirled, to bellow his orders for'ard. 'Weather braces! Ready about!'

Now Boatswain Sturgee's voice rose, up there for'ard as men flung themselves to the braces on the starboard side. The Master snapped, 'Helm a-lee! *Hard*, now!'

Down below there by the whipstaff they were already passing on Langhorne's quick order for all the starboard pieces to give fire, and now Joss Wenman's roar took that up as one of the unseen Quartermasters sang out acknowledgement to Pennyfeather's helm direction. A roar of cheering throughout the gun-decks swallowed the end of it: here on the quarter-deck all eyes watched as the hubbub rose below and on the upper decks men raced to man the braces and the fore-sail sheets. And, staring upwards at the topsails then, they saw them tremble, flap, flutter and fall limp for lack of wind: *Revenge* lost way at once, the hiss of the sea lessening in their ears as she slowed before her prow had even started its ordered swing to starboard. Below, the gunners still cheered as touch-holes spurted fire and fumes: but their galleon was at a standstill, now, becalmed in the lee of the towering *San Felipe*; three times *Revenge*'s size, she blocked the wind entirely.

As the truth bore home into the minds behind those watching eyes, *Revenge* seemed to explode in one vast thunderclap that was a full broadside of the starboard batteries: her decks heaved, the ship rocked violently to port, black powder-smoke streaked with orange flame and flying crimson sparks swept up and across her decks. As the smoke thinned and cleared, Langhorne watched the Spaniard; saw his bulwarks shattered at the waist, his foremast swaying, crashing down across his prow, his mainsail shredded, blown out in lively streamers on the wind. On his decks dozens of men were down, live men struggling, panic-stricken, out of heaps of dead; Spanish screams were drowned only by the cheers of English gunners. A black hole gaped below his fo'c'sle, linking two gun-ports in that upper tier, and inside the rent timbers Langhorne saw the spreading orange glow of fire.

He thought, If, by now, we were near about to the other tack, to give him that again from our other side, one hard below close upon another . . . Ah, *if*!

By such 'if's', battles were won or lost: men lived, or died . . .

VII

And while now the great San Philip hung above us like a cloud,
Whence the thunderbolt will fall
Long and loud,
Four galleons drew away
From the Spanish fleet that day,
And two upon the larboard and two upon the starboard lay,
And the battle-thunder broke from them all.

Tennyson
(The *Revenge*: A Ballad of the Fleet)

Through the last eddies of the choking gunsmoke Penny-feather stared at Grenville. The Master had the look of a bull, baffled by some obstacle that had sprung up to check his charge: a maddened bull, goaded beyond his own comprehension, even beyond rage.

He stood and stared, dumb in his bewilderment, his hands loose and open at his sides; he opened his mouth to speak, closed it again, his jaw-muscles bunching and the veins swelling on his neck; his hands moved, spread apart from his sides, folded again limp against his cord-cloth breeches. They were thick, square hands, richly haired along their backs; they'd hauled on a thousand ropes, grasped a thousand spars; they'd struck men down when there'd been need for that, and for years now for all their strength and bluntness they'd used and adjusted the delicate instruments of navigation. Now, for the first time in his life, they felt useless to him . . .

Grenville spoke sharply, as if the Master's perplexity was something that annoyed him. 'Sling your yards, Master. Douse your fore-sail.' He jerked his head impatiently towards the approaching Spaniard. 'Spread your mariners to repel boarders.'

Pennyfeather swung round, bawling for a messenger, and

the two seamen boys detailed for that duty came scrambling simultaneously up the port and starboard ladders. He pointed at the nearer of them, Maine, who was heaving his loutish body on to the quarter-deck's starboard side.

'One's enough! *You*, boy!'

Langhorne shouted, 'Hold, there! You – Wenman!' He beckoned, a quick sweep of his left hand that brought the other boy, Jonno Wenman, running aft again, stumbling as he turned. Langhorne's other hand gripped the hilt of his sword – an English rapier, long and with two cutting edges, not the new Spanish rapier that had a blade like a whip so that only the point served for killing – already unsheathed; its heavy blade was a broad streak of silver in the afternoon sun.

Well – near-evening: that sun was dropping, now, towards the horizon in the west.

Pennyfeather told Wally Maine: 'Run to the Boatswain. Tell him – sling topsail yards: douse fore-sail: then—' he glanced at Langhorne, and the soldier nodded quickly. 'Then take pikes, defend the ship. Go!' Langhorne turned to Jonno Wenman as Maine ran for'ard taking that starboard ladder in a single, flying leap.

Jonno looked ridiculous in a seaman's leather jerkin that reached to near his knees. Langhorne told him, 'Run to your father, boy. Tell him we stand and fight: to engage the Spaniards as they come. You hear me?'

Young Wenman repeated the message in a fast gabble in his high, child's voice. Langhorne studied his face for signs of fear; but the boy looked more lost than frightened. Langhorne thought, He's too young to be away from his mother, let alone at sea. The child was running for'ard now, and smoke drifting in clouds across the deck hid his thin back as he reached the ladder and started down it. That smoke came from *Revenge*'s upper gun-deck where the guns fired ceaselessly, singly and in twos and threes or now and then by quarters, as they were loaded and brought ready; thin smoke drifted down, too, from the Spaniard, from light guns in his high castles and from the fire that still burnt or smouldered below his fo'c'sle; but his main armament was still silent,

112

waiting, incalculable menace in the dark jutting muzzles of the rows of cannon.

The lower port-side battery was still held ready, and the starboard pieces on the same deck were also now reloaded, primed and run out. Joss Wenman peered anxiously through one of the steerage ports on the windward side, where the fowler which used that port had just fired and now was being cleared – wormed – and re-charged by its two-man crew (the piece weighed only 750 pounds) and he saw the great bulk of the *San Felipe* drawing slowly nearer, obliterating any view of other Spanish ships close by; she was already within crossbow-shot and from here he could distinguish the features of soldiers in her waist where they lined the bulwarks, see noses and dark beards below burnished helmets and those helmets turning, flashing in the sunlight as their wearers turned their heads to survey *Revenge*'s decks, castles and rigging; they laughed among themselves as they pointed out features of the English galleon, laughed in loud contempt as they pointed aloft at the Royal Arms and the cross of Saint George. The Master Gunner gritted his teeth and told himself, I hold my fire for nothing, this galleon's still not swinging as she was meant to be and now she'll not, she's still, and those monkeys in their armour come to board! He saw the long triple lines of the Spanish guns and realized that at any moment they'd dispatch a broadside from all three tiers, such a smash of shot as a galleon of this *Revenge*'s size could barely hope to stand against: and here he waited with his own heavy cannon primed and idle when every instinct told him they should be firing as fast as they could be worked, getting in first with the blows that counted most, the early ones, the blows that pulverized, threw gunners (Spanish gunners anyway) into panic and disorder, shattered guns, set fires in powder-stores and lockers—

With a grunt of explosive rage, flinging himself back from the open port as the fowler screeched forward on its straining tackles, Wenman dived headlong for the square of hatchway; he shouted, 'Below there! Rowan!'

'Yea!'

113

Below him in the gloom of 'tween-decks Alec Rowan's dark face was upturned to this filtered light; there was anger in it as well as eagerness. The Master Gunner bellowed above the sound of steady cannonade, 'All your starboard, give fire! All your port, by quarters, fire as they bear!'

'Yea yea!' The acknowledgement was a cry or joy, a welcome to release. Cheers filled the tight-packed low-roofed gun-decks as powder spluttered at the touch-holes of culverins, demi-cannon and cannon-periers, and Rowan's voice moved for'ard, roaring orders. As he went up again, his ears and brain ready and steeled against concussion, Joss Wenman heard the distinctive roar of a port-piece firing from its position in the Great Cabin aft; he climbed on, ducked inside the steerage compartment, brushed past some anonymous figure cluttering his path as he hurried to that fowler's port again. As he reached it the lower broadside and the periers crashed out, a ripple of hard thunder that swept *Revenge*'s decks while black powder smoke and flame flung out and up and flew back in the wind; before the smoke closed in front of him, shutting off his view of the Spaniard, he had a moment's glimpse of the slaughter wrought by the ten pounds of grape-shot from that port-piece aft in Grenville's quarters, the complacent, jeering ranks of soldiers shattered, flung about the enemy's waist, some running for the hatchways, others writhing where they'd dropped. But then the smoke enveloped him; he turned inboard, coughing violently, fingering his smarting eyes and slapping at something that burnt his neck; in the sudden reeking dark his son was calling, high and thin,

'Cap'n Lang'n says, sir, we stand an' fight an' you to fire your guns as Spaniards come! From the Cap'n, that's his word, sir!'

Smoke clearing now – and the Master Gunner's hands gripped his son's thin, shrinking shoulders. The message – well, that was done already, seen to, it went over his head like the drifting, thinning smoke; Joss Wenman barely heard it as he searched for a clear sight of his son's eyes and felt himself bursting with an inner pressure, a need for words, for such contact as they'd not shared before or needed. He felt a passion rising in him: it had something to do with the boy's white face, the eyes that belonged in another, land-bound world, belonged to his wife, this boy's mother, who'd not wanted him to come; it had something to do with this crescendo of sound and fire and danger in which certainly those eyes had no place, or should have had none. He felt that rising – risen – force of emotion, empathy and guilt, and he gripped the boy's shoulders in their loose leather covering and shouted, bending to put his broad, bearded face close to the sharp, pale one, 'Why, Jonno – *Jonno!* Ah, by damn, I'd—'

The boy had twisted like an eel and leapt back, jerking his shoulders free of the weight of his father's hands; below them the guns fired again, thunder and flame now in control, possession, noise and blackness streaked with brilliance and roofed with sunlight obliterating reason, thought; through slowly clearing gun-smoke Wenman saw that his son had gone.

He dragged himself back to that starboard port, remembering that as yet he'd seen nothing of the effects of that broadside of his heavier guns, hoping there'd be signs by now that the Spaniard had been damaged especially around the waterline.

But the *San Felipe* was now so close that he saw only the wall of timber that was her larboard side, pierced with three rows of cannon but towering so much above *Revenge* that from here he couldn't see anything of her upper decks; he saw shot-wounds in her side, holes and cracked and shattered timbers; the length of her stretched away to his left and right so that neither her bow nor her stern was in his view, only this great looming fortress, a fortress whose guns (even as he stared at her now and heard from above, between the bursts of shooting, the high commands in Spanish from her decks) delivered their first full shattering broadside, at point-blank range.

Revenge's starboard bulwarks were lined with crouching

115

men who waited under that partial cover to meet the on-slaught of the Spanish troops. They knelt and squatted on decks already scarred and pitted with Spanish shot, while marksmen placed all through the ship but particularly in the high parts of the fo'c'sle and aftercastle and in the fighting tops kept up a hot and ceaseless fire at the ranks of soldiers on the decks of the *San Felipe;* arquebuses, muskets and cross-bows filled the air with the noise of firing and the whine of missiles; the enemy, too, crouched against their bulwarks and held close to other cover, but there were so many of them that the English marksmen were never short of targets.

Grenville squatted close by the top of the starboard quar-ter-deck ladder, his eyes on a level with the bulwark; sword in hand, he watched the Spaniard closing, and from here too he could look down for'ard across the half-deck and into the waist, where men waited not only against the bulwarks but also in two high nests of cable near the centre, only the ends of their pikes visible above the rims of rope.

The cloth 'fights' had been mostly shot away by now, and trailed in rags across the bulwarks.

Grenville was watching the Spaniard, judging the moment to order his trumpeter to sound-off, to have the men stand-to and the bombs hurled across the narrow strip of water, when the whole of the *San Felipe*'s side erupted in a great sheet of flame and smoke that leapt from bow to stern, bul-warks to waterline. Reeling back, instinctively ducking his head, his first reaction was mostly pure surprise: he'd reckoned that as they'd held their fire this long their inten-tion must surely be to spare *Revenge* any heavy damage, in order to have her intact as a prize . . .

Surprise was drowned in horror as *Revenge* took that full broadside in her oaken belly. By the sound and feel of it, the whole of her starboard side must have been smashed: and as he waited, his ears filled with the sounds of rending timbers and screaming, dying men while smoke swirled round so thickly that he couldn't see even Langhorne who was within arm's reach – or had been, a few seconds ago – he heard the mizen rigging parting up there above his head. Looking up

116

quickly into clearer air, he saw – against a sky that was already dimming and streaking with the early stages of Atlantic sunset – the mizen-mast sway and shiver and fall back, trailing ropes that snapped and danced in the air around it; falling, topsail and topsail yard and all the encumbrance of broken rigging, it looked huge, bigger than life-size: but as it crashed down across the starboard quarter, narrowly missing the round-house, renewed firing from *Revenge*'s starboard batteries drowned the sound of its fall.

At deck level the smoke was still thick, but he could see Langhorne now, close to him, facing aft, coughing into the powder fumes. Grenville grabbed the soldier's arm.

'See to the bombs, now, have them thrown. Nay – is Gawdy by you?'

'Here, sir.' Langhorne's hand was on Philip Gawdy's shoulder. Grenville moved up beside them both.

'Philip. Go aft there, while these fumes still hide us, have the bombs thrown on that Spaniard's decks. See to it quickly, lad.'

Gawdy nodded, and vanished aft, into the deeper smoke. Grenville stood erect, watching the Spaniard's shrouded, looming shape. He wanted those bombs over *now*, this minute, to disrupt the ranks of soldiers just when they'd be on the point of boarding. The smoke was thinning fast. Langhorne shouted in his ear,

'Mainmast's gone, Sir Richard!'

He turned, and saw in renewed surprise that what the soldier said was true – or nearly true. The main topmast had gone, and the fighting top, and the upper part of that lower spar; the stump still standing was charred and jagged at its top. It must have happened, of course, when the full broadside had hit and there'd been so much noise and smoke that he'd not heard or seen its fall. Now the topmast lay with its shattered lower part in the waist-deck and its end protruding over the port side, canted high in the air where it rested on the break of the fo'c'sle. The topsail itself, and a maze of tangled rigging, trailed to the sea in swathes and streamers of charred rope and canvas.

Grenville glanced at the pikemen closest to him; his eyes

rested on a short, wiry fellow whose black hair held streaks of grey.

'You, fellow – your name?'

'My – why, Clayborn, sir! Dick Clayborn—'

Grenville clapped him on his leathered shoulder. 'Well, Dick, I'd have you climb that stump there for me!'

With his other hand he was pointing at the standing remains of the mainmast, and the mariner's eyes widened in surprise. But a grin still lingered on his face, at the Vice-Admiral's use of his Christian name.

'First get a hammer and some nails. Then cut loose our Sovereign's standard from that tangle there – and up with you, and nail it where it should be. Well?'

'Aye aye!' Clayborn's grin was one of pure delight. Grenville had already turned away; the *San Felipe* was near aboard them now, soldiers poised along his bulwarks. Those bulwarks visibly shook as *Revenge*'s heavy ordnance let loose another salvo; for all the damage that last Spanish broadside must have done – though the fact that men were still working those lower starboard guns was in itself re-assuring – a much greater weight of English shot must by now have bored its way into the Spaniard's vitals. He'd be sore below, for all those soldiers posturing on his decks!

'Trumpeter – *sound*!'

As the lad raised his bugle Grenville heard a series of loud, thumping explosions from the Spaniard's stern. Those were the bombs; and well timed. They'd take care, nearly enough, of the Spanish after-guard . . .

The trumpet call swept up clearly, a high bronze note above the sounds of battle. All along *Revenge*'s side the pikemen rose, cheering, to meet the Spanish onslaught. But Grenville, at the after end of the half-deck now, frowned as he stared across at those ranks of soldiers; there were too many of them for his own tiny force of sailors to withstand for long. He roared, 'Bombs! Have we no bombs here?'

'Yea, here, sir! Here!' John Creed appeared beside him, an evil-looking jar-grenade in each of his wide hands. The Boatswain's Mate called over his shoulder, 'The match then, Jabez! Jabez Shaw! *Damn*, where'd—'

A little, dark man, whom Grenville remembered seeing with Creed ashore during the embarkation of the sick, had sprung forward with a burning slow-match in his hand. Grenville remembered him because of his striking ugliness: he was short, broad, and from his strangely curved shoulders hung arms as long as an ape's. That monkey-look was all the more evident when he was seen beside John Creed, who was easily the biggest man in the ship's company, tall, straight and thick-chested. It occurred to Grenville that this Jabez Shaw might at any moment spring jabbering on to one of his big friend's shoulders . . .

But Creed held out his bombs, and the ape-man, grinning and breathing hard, touched his match to the fused neck of each in turn. When they were well alight, the Boatswain's Mate nodded at his hunched assistant, turned with his eyes still on the smoking stems of fuse, and hurled the bombs one after the other into the centre of the mob of soldiers in the Spaniard's waist.

They fell in showers of sparks and a trail of smoke from each smouldering fuse; they bounced on gleaming helmets and on steel-armoured shoulders, thence thudded to the deck; the nearer soldiers, panic-stricken, fought wildly against those around them in their efforts to escape. Roars of laughter rose from the English watchers, Grenville himself so overcome with mirth at the Spaniards' antics that he had to bend and clasp his stomach with the pain of it: that mob of soldiers seethed, faces turned upwards with mouths wide open in screams of fear and protest: weapons flashed, men broke free and ran, to be met in the clearer parts of the deck by officers who halted them and drove them back at sword point. But even as the bombs exploded within a second of each other, cutting deep swathes of dead and wounded around the places where they'd dropped, a Spanish trumpet blared from the enemy quarter-deck; a Spanish soldier in full armour sprang on to the *San Felipe*'s bulwark waving his fellows up to join him, yelling some challenge, no doubt offensive, in his own tongue across the yard of water which was all that now separated the two ships. Then he jumped, hurling himself directly at the lines of pikes, breaking

119

through, falling to his knees, rising again and turning; pikemen at *Revenge*'s side whirled to engage him, and as they turned other Spaniards leapt across, trusting their armour to deflect the pikes, forcing a gap through which it seemed now in the heat of it that half a Spanish regiment was pouring . . .

Seeing the growing menace, Grenville raised his sword and took a pace towards the head of the ladder; but Langhorne, who'd been watching over the ship's side, called to him urgently. 'Sir Richard! Look, sir!'

Checking with his left hand already on the ladder's rail and the light of battle in his narrowed eyes, Grenville shouted angrily over his shoulder, 'What? You'd stay me, Captain?'

'The Spaniard's *going*, sir!'

The *San Felipe* had swung in under rudder, turning to place herself where she wanted, the galleon still swinging and with wind behind her high castles which held it almost as well as sails. In the confusion of the bombs' explosions here and at the stern, and in the steady rain of shot and arrows, the Spanish sailors had skimped their duty and grappled with only a single rope; and as their ship surged and swung, that rope had strained and parted so that the ships' sterns moved apart, now, their prows just kissing and then they too parting, a gap of water growing between the whole lengths of the ships, *Revenge* still immobile, *San Felipe* still under way and with that swing to port, dropping down to leeward past *Revenge*'s bow.

No more of her soldiers could follow into *Revenge*; and those dozen who'd crossed – now that there was time to count, it came to no more than that – could not get back. Several were already down; cheering wildly, pikemen ringed the survivors, driving them steadily back towards the bulwarks and the sea.

Grenville looked almost disappointed as he lowered his sword-arm and detachedly watched the battle in which there was now no need for him to join. Then the Master, Pennyfeather, shattered the unexpected calm.

'To larboard, sir! They board to larboard!'

A second 'Apostle', the galleon *San Bernabé* of Bilbao, flagship of the Biscayans, had slid downwind under the English stern and now, having checked and hauled his wind, was driving up under streaming banners to lay aboard *Revenge*'s larboard side.

Yet that voice now hailing was not in Spanish: the words were English, and touched with Devonshire at that! Grenville, who with the others at his heels had rushed to the port bulwarks of the half-deck, stared in amazement that turned quickly to delight: beyond that Spanish bow, downwind by a cable's length or more, the English victualler, the *George Noble*, was beating up to her Vice-Admiral's assistance. Her Captain hailed again.

'*Revenge*, ahoy! Your orders, sir!'

For one moment Grenville hesitated. Then, cupping his hands to his mouth, he hailed back: 'Save yourself! Leave me to my fortune!'

He'd lowered his hands, and stood irresolute: now he raised them again and bellowed, 'Cut your mainsail! *Go!*'

On the *George Noble*'s quarter-deck a man standing alone removed his hat and waved it towards *Revenge*. His words came faintly to them across the water:

'God be with you!'

Grenville kept his back to Langhorne and the others, and he made no comment; but he watched the victualler closely until she'd swung away and loosed her sails to run before the wind.

Joss Wenman, Master Gunner, leant back against the mainmast in the upper gun-deck and closed his eyes quickly to protect them against flying sparks as the starboard cannon-periers fired; the heavy pieces flung back past him close on either side, the breechings jarred and sang and the trucks jerked up and pounded at the deck where strewn sawdust was now sodden with men's blood. Blindly in the smoke he urged the gun's crew on, to worm, sponge out, reload, haul back their pieces to the ports.

'Then hold your fire, lads.'

He dragged his forearm slowly across his eyes, wiping away the sweat that ran down with grime and powder in it so that much of the time he was half-blind; through eyes now barely open he focused on smoke that swirled and patterned in the broad shafts of light that flooded through the gun-ports, and in the narrower, irregular spears of brilliance which thrust through shot holes, through innumerable gaps blasted in that starboard side.

He'd never seen a ship quite so badly hurt in a single broadside.

Joss Wenman was Master Gunner by warrant; but he was Gunner's Mate, too, for Alec Rowan was dead, flattened against the port-side timbers of the lower gun-deck when one of the for'ard culverins had broken its breechings in recoil and careered right through the deck, killing Rowan and two of the opposite culverin's crew at the same time, though one of those was not yet dead, in fact. There were too many hurt and dying to have them carried to the Chirurgeon, and the men who might have carried them were needed at the guns in place of others who were dead.

He was Quarter Gunner, too, three times over. From this deck only one of them remained alive – Thomas Glinn – and now Wenman had sent him down to take charge of the lower deck, acting as Gunner's Mate. Down there it was a shambles, a butcher's shop: the urine tubs were dry and the men were using salt water in their sponges, but they could as easily have used blood. The decks stank of it, and the deck-head dripped.

In truth he'd one gun's crew to each pair of guns, but by spreading them, thinning the crews, he could man two guns out of three; and once the guns were loaded and in position in the ports and primed, it needed only one man to fire each piece. Replenishing, and hauling outboard: that was the harder part.

The dead had been dragged amidships, out of the way of the living; and there was a group of dying, sprawled up by the foremast between the for'ard sakers and the demi-culverins of the bow-chase. Those were the dying, not the wounded; the wounded worked the guns.

Among the dead was Robert Drax, Yeoman of the shot-room; but there was no yeoman needed, now, since the store was empty and the shot that lay in the lockers at the guns was all that remained to fire. Well, those lockers were well up, most of them; *Revenge* had plenty of bite left in her. She'd give some back . . .

He'd come aft, and over to the larboard side, and he was helping to haul the two sakers there back into their ports. All that port battery was reloaded now, since they'd lacked targets in the past half-hour and Wenman had been using their crews as reinforcements on the starboard guns; but now from those after ports the prow and forepart of an approaching galleon was seen in the failing light, dark against a shining, dusk-streaked sea; she was steering close, as the other had, doubtless with intent to board.

(Below here, he'd heard and felt the boarding by the *San Felipe*. The crunch of timbers meeting as the Spaniard touched alongside: the crashes of armoured men landing heavily on the deck above: the pounding feet, the bugle and the clash of arms. But half consciously, and all that in a dream, happening not on the deck above his head, but in another world, a separate life inhabited by a different breed of man: reality had been here, where for a time it had been hard to know who was living and who dead, whether his own blindness was permanent, whether a man could drown in the blood of other men: reality had been nightmare, in those minutes.)

Wenman stood back as the last saker ran hard into its port; he freed the powder-horn from his belt, and moving round behind the guns he primed both touch-holes. Their crews, squatting on the slippery deck, leaning against the ship's side between their pieces, watched him dazedly out of eyes that were bloodshot slits in masks of soot; the men were stripped to the waist, some completely naked; the sweat ran down in streams and blood ran too, and men rubbed powder in their wounds to staunch it.

He hurried for'ard again, to the midship ports of the

cannon-periers, and squinted along the barrel of the fore-most. As he'd expected, the prow of the closing Spaniard was just coming level with it. Wenman grunted to himself, nodding slowly; he watched for a moment longer, then stepped back and straightened.

'You there to starboard – man these pieces! Sharp, now!' The perier crews came over, silent, knowing the time for grumbling was gone, and slumped beside the larboard guns. Abaft them, the demi-culverin and the two sakers were already manned. Wenman told these fellows, 'When ye've given fire here, get for'ard – sakers see? – ay, and give fire smartly as they bear. Then serve all afresh, without my order. D'ye hear?'

They nodded, speechless still, having no breath to waste. Wenman edged back until the pin-rail pressed against his thighs, put up a hand to rest it where the mainmast pierced the deck above. He shouted,

'All larboard pieces – give fire!'

Again that thunder, fire and smoke, acrid stench, the roar and racket of recoil: and as it died, and stilled, so that now he could hear the sea outside the hull and feet pounding the deck above and a cry out there in the daylight, a cry drowned at once in the distant, impersonal rattle of musket fire, while the smoke still hung heavy, almost motionless, reeking in the fetid gun-deck, he stood where he was in the blackness tasting grit and gunpowder and the smell of blood in his throat and nostrils, waiting to be certain that all the guns had fired before he started aft behind their trucks, and he heard the movements and hard breathing of the men as they dragged themselves back to the ordnance to start it all over again: worm, sponge, ream . . . But from up for'ard he heard that voice again, babbling about water to a woman it called *Judith, love* . . . He couldn't recognize the voice.

The Master Gunner wiped his eyes again along his fore-arm; he pushed himself away from the mast and stumbled aft, stopping once to peer out through a gun-port at the still closing Spaniard; he showed no signs of damage. Well, likely *Revenge* would show none, on this larboard side, except above decks.

He clambered down through the hatchway, into the lower gun-deck. It was darker here, for no light filtered from above now; Wenman turned for'ard, peering through the smoky gloom.

'Glinn? Tom Glinn there?'

'Yea.' Thomas Glinn was experienced and skilled enough to have been a Master Gunner himself by now; probably he would have been, if it wasn't for his taste for drink. But he was sober enough now; he was stooping, for he was a tall man, peering into Joss Wenman's face through the deck's close stink and fog. He growled, 'Ay, I've seen him, Devil rot his filthy soul!' Wenman blinked in surprise: then, at the next words, realized he was referring to the Spaniard. 'Larboard broadside's ready, Joss. Chain-shot amidships.'

'All?'

'All ready, ay.'

'Do all bear, Tom?'

Glinn swivelled his long, bent body around and shouted into the deeper gloom up for'ard – the light that seeped into the gun-ports was fainter now as dusk set in – 'You for'ard culverins! D'you bear?'

'Aye aye!'

Wenman grunted. On the upper gun-deck that he'd just left, the two for'ard sakers on the port side fired; well then, all right, those culverins *did* bear. He pushed past Glinn, led him for'ard past the trucks of the demi-cannon, the guns that held the chain-shot. The two men stopped beside the base of the mainmast, and Joss Wenman croaked harshly,

'All your larboard, now – *give fire!*'

General Don Martin Bertendona, who at this moment was bringing his great Biscayan galleon *San Bernabé* up to lay aboard *Revenge*'s port side, had an account to settle with this little English warship. It was an account dating not from the Armada – although he'd met her there as well – but from only two years back, and so fresh in his memory that the thought of it still rankled as a personal affront. For

Revenge had swaggered into Corunna in 1589 with Francis Drake aboard her, and Martin Bertendona had been forced to the ignominy of setting fire to his own galleon as the only alternative to capture.

It seemed to him now that Fate had arranged this turning of the tables: *Revenge* lay helpless, isolated and immobile, already badly damaged and entirely at his mercy, very different from the insufferably jaunty little ship he'd seen darting into action in the Channel in 1588, flaunting her banners inside a Spanish harbour the year after!

General Bertendona looked down at *Revenge* lying there inert and doomed; he thought of the 500 soldiers packing the decks of this new, 1,500-ton *San Bernabé*, and he smiled grimly to himself as he watched the distance narrowing . . .

On *Revenge*'s waist-deck half the number of Spanish soldiers who'd been marooned there when the *San Felipe* had sheered off had been cut down; the rest were still on their feet and fighting, but they were tired, outnumbered, slowing, hemmed in by pikemen, straddling their fallen comrades as they fought.

Now one of them saw the *San Bernabé* looming close; he shouted the news as he warded off the thrust of a pike, and at the same moment soldiers on that high fo'c'sle as it towered past with only a few yards between the two ships' sides saw them fighting for their lives inside the English circle, and cheered them loudly, shrieking encouragement and promises of aid. The English turned in surprise to glance over their shoulders at the approaching galleon, and the soldiers seized advantage of that distraction to drive forward in a body, swords swinging, thrusting, stepping inside the lengths of the pikes so that the pikemen had to retreat to keep their enemies at bay; pike-heads rang on steel armour as the Spaniards, elated, pressed forward again and faster, fighting a way towards the port-side bulwarks where their friends' arrival was plainly imminent. One more went down, a pike-head in his throat, the shaft of the pike breaking as he fell, his own sword finishing its swing and embedding itself in the deck between his assailant's feet. But suddenly the Spaniards as if by prior or telepathic agreement switched the direction of their attack, swinging to the right, outflanking and confusing the English sailors; a short, hard rush, and they gained the bulwarks just as the *San Bernabé*'s timbers scrunched against *Revenge*'s rubbing strake.

Grappling irons flew, fell and locked the ships together, the Spaniard alongside all of *Revenge*'s forepart and over-lapping her prow; below, gun-fire blazed intermittently so that the vessels shuddered in each others' embrace while smoke and sparks welled up above their decks; above, arrows and bullets whined while muskets and arquebuses crashed incessantly.

The five surviving Spaniards flung themselves over the bulwarks into Bertendona's ship; they were at once engulfed in a cheering crowd of their own people. The English drew back into cover, disengaging slowly, cautiously, under a rain of small-arms fire, leaving that waist-deck littered with their own and Spanish dead, with broken pikes and shattered swords. As the last glow of sunset died in the Spaniard's topsails and night spread its dark, impervious shroud across the sea, the two fighting ships lay locked together with empty decks. Below, the gunners still moved about the ord-nance, and the guns fired sporadically, making thunder be-neath the feet of men who waited and watched in the fo'c'sles and aftercastles, at gun-ports and embrasures; they watched over deserted decks, scarred and littered stretches of blood-stained timber which for the moment were no-man's-lands; the Spaniards, who with their hundreds of fresh men and reserves of ammunition held the initiative, were waiting presumably for some moment of special ad-vantage, perhaps for moonrise, perhaps even for daylight; the English kept themselves awake and staunched their wounds as best they could, counted their living and held their fire, held themselves ready to meet the assault when-ever it should come.

It was coming; but not, initially, from Bertendona. In the dark astern the great *San Cristobal*, flagship of General Don Marcos de Arumburu who commanded the squadron of

Castille, had at last won up to windward; she'd turned her bowsprit towards *Revenge* and now slid closer, huge and silent and so far unobserved, the sea hissing along her sides and her fo'c'sle crammed with soldiers.

VIII

And the sun went down, and the stars came out far over the
summer sea,
But never a moment ceased the fight of the one and the fifty-three.
Ship after ship, the whole night long, their high-built galleons came,
Ship after ship, the whole night long, with her battle-thunder and
flame;
Ship after ship, the whole night long, drew back with her dead
and her shame.
For some were sunk and many were shatter'd, and so could fight
us no more—
God of battles, was ever a battle like this in the world before?
                                                    Tennyson
                          (The *Revenge*: A Ballad of the Fleet)

Gun-flash squared the port in sudden orange flame, and in
its light Philip Gawdy saw Grenville briefly in half-profile;
Sir Richard was watching the Spaniard as he spoke to Langhorne, and from near by one of the bases in the after cubbridge head had sent off two rounds quickly, a fast rat-tat,
aimed no doubt at some movement in the waist, perhaps a
Spaniard approaching the *San Bernabé*'s bulwarks. Below,
another gun fired, shaking the deck they stood on, and again
Grenville's lean, bearded profile was thrown up in sharp
momentary relief against lurid colour as the echoes of the
gun-shot faded and the ball crashed home in Bertendona's
galleon.

Gawdy heard him say quietly, bitterly, 'If I'd more men—'
'Aye.' Langhorne, close to Grenville at that port, sighed
agreement. With more men, they could have taken the
offensive: at least, moved to cut the *San Bernabé* adrift. As
it was, circumstances forced them to be patient, to lie doggo
under cover (they were in the Great Cabin, its for'ard part,
near the steps that led down into the steerage and so out to

the waist) and await attack, conserve their small force in readiness for that.

Guns crashed out again somewhere below their feet, and almost at once the Spaniard answered with a furious broadside that lit her towering stern, showed for an instant one bearded, helmeted face out-thrust at an open, carved embrasure, and the jutting barrels of muskets at a dozen others; *Revenge* shuddered, trembled as she took fresh hurt below; then the port-piece at the after end of this Great Cabin belched its load of grape-shot at the Spanish aftercastle, the gunner no doubt hoping to include that incautious watcher in his spread of victims. The noise of the discharge, in this confined space, was terrible: Gawdy's ears sang as if there were wires strung across inside his head, and he stood rooted, helpless, useless, bewildered and inactive, his eyes wide open to the fire-streaked darkness, to the ringing hell of battle that had nothing of glory in it, none of the triumph and excitement he'd dreamed of in past months. He'd heard Langhorne, a few minutes ago, report to Grenville that from a rough count he reckoned one half of the men who'd been unhurt two hours ago were now dead: they'd sailed with just 100 fit, so there were fifty now left to defend the ship – to defend, rather, what had been a ship but was rapidly becoming a hulk.

And waterlogged, at that. Gawdy had heard Langhorne, back from his tour of inspection below decks, telling that sculptured stone profile that hardly moved at all except sometimes to raise one hand and shield his eyes against the more brilliant flashes of the guns, that the Carpenter had reported three shot-holes below the waterline. The Carpenter and his Mates had stopped them, but only temporarily and lightly; the men were still down there, trying to make a surer job of it and at the same time watching for new wounds in the bottom timbers, working in several feet of water in the hold where only those of the sick who'd been able to muster enough strength to sit, or crouch, were still alive. The others were no longer sick, but drowned, their limp bodies awash in the pitch dark, low-decked compartment.

Gawdy had heard all that, and he'd heard too Langhorne's report on the state of the gun-decks, where Joss Wenman was driving a handful of surviving gunners from one piece to another to serve and fire them as best he could at targets offered; he'd heard it all, and had recurring now that sensation of unreality, the feeling that none of this was true. Well – his arm flamed from the stab and slash of a glancing Spanish arrow: *that* was real: what was impossible to accept was the hopelessness of it, the certainty of defeat and death. If it were true and real, how in heaven's name could Grenville, who had a family to return to, great estates to administer, wealth and position to enjoy, stand like a graven image and speak without a tremble in his voice, without even a suggestion of dismay? Speak as though *Revenge*, in this fight or rather slaughter, had at least an even chance?

'What, Master? *What* d'you say?'

That quiet, rumbling voice, then, had been Pennyfeather's. It said again now, out of the dark over there at the ship's side, 'Before the light went, sir, while you were still amidships or near there and myself on the quarter-deck and the Dons were boarding – well, at that time, sir, the *Foresight* came – I think to our assistance.'

'Came? *Foresight*?'

'Yea, sir. I'd but a sight of her, for she held in the wind, and there were Spaniards thick there to the east of us and in between. They drove her off: but I saw her guns fire more than once.' The Master's cough was a raucous sound in the dark. 'That's all, Sir Richard. You'd have wished to know it.'

'Ay.' Again the guns' roar, the brilliance of their flame; etched black against it, Grenville had turned to face Pennyfeather's voice. He said, '*Foresight*. Ay – Captain Vavasour. A gentleman whom I shall live, I hope, to thank for his endeavours—'

The cry that drowned his words was loud and urgent and it came from only a few feet away.

'*Aft here – larboard quarter—!*'

That musketeer had no need to say more: no time: the impact of the *San Cristobal*'s prow running against their quarter was a heavy thud, a protesting creak of straining groaning timbers, *Revenge* jolting, quivering, rocking to starboard: men were flung headlong, falling in heaps, the air thick with curses and shouts of alarm, Langhorne's orders piercing the general noise. Out there in the dark a Spanish bugle blared, and Spanish voices screamed excited challenge. Men were leaping from the newcomer's prow to land thudding on *Revenge*'s quarter-deck—

For Gawdy, disengaging himself frantically from a knot of struggling, shouting men in the dark, tilted cabin, the bedlam around him and the alarm above marked the beginning of hours of chaos in which it seemed, looking back on it afterwards, that he lost his own identity and power of thought and with that his sense of fear: he was part of a mob that followed Grenville, followed Langhorne, blindly, answering shout for shout while gun-fire dazed him and deafened him and choking smoke engulfed him and the sword in his hand had a life of its own which ignored the deadened, burning muscles in the arm that wielded it. He was part of a rush of men who flung themselves growling like wild animals out into the waist and up the ladders to the half-deck: across that and up again to the quarter-deck which was filling with armoured, cheering Spanish soldiers who'd already cut the ship's ensign from her quarter-staff. They met head-on, Grenville roaring continuously *'England, and Saint George! Saint George for England!'* in a tone of wild exultation and exuberant joy. Behind Grenville Langhorne echoed the same words, and the sailors sweeping forward bellowed them in chorus, and Gawdy found them in his own throat too although they never reached his ears which were filled with the sound of steel that clashed on steel, pounding feet and the crash of guns and small-arms. Musketeers and bowmen in the *San Bernabé* had poured shot into the backs of the English as they flowed up the ladders from the waist on to the poop decks, and many had fallen to those bullets before they reached the invading Spaniards, and Gawdy himself had been hit again and Langhorne too, and in a sudden, brilliant lightning from the guns he'd seen Pennyfeather, the Master, covered in blood

132

from head to foot and roaring like a bull as with a group of men that included Sturgee, the Boatswain, he'd charged into the Spaniards' flank, felling men in droves before his rush was halted and a danger of encirclement forced him back into the line of men that Grenville led: Sturgee had lost an ear.

Once they'd got up there on the quarter-deck the *San Bernabé*'s marksmen held their fire, unable to distinguish Englishman from Spaniard in the wild mêlée that met sword to sword across the width of the ship. Grenville still yelled his battle-cry and at least as many Spaniards fell as English, but Gawdy was aware, vaguely, that he and the men with him were being driven slowly backwards under the weight of numbers: thirty men faced 300 and his sword had broken, shattered on Spanish armour, he'd another now, taken from the deck, its hilt sticky and slippery with blood. Below, the guns still fired, and as the English evacuated their quarter-deck to form a new defensive line across the half-deck, the glow of a steady fire illuminated *Revenge*'s port quarter, grew brighter so that Spanish soldiers pouring down the ladders on either side were thrown up in stark silhouette against what was now undoubtedly flame, flames on the Spaniard's fo'c's'le, and now as Gawdy still edged back in the line of English swords and pikes, stumbling sometimes on the bodies of men who'd fallen to musket shots and arrows on their way along this deck minutes earlier, some of them groaning and calling out for aid which no man had time to give them, as he fell back inch by shuffling, stabbing inch and to his right front Grenville's sword was a darting, thrusting, whirling shaft of silver against those flames, the first of the explosions started in the Spanish prow.

The first was small: a thud, and a shower of burning timber splinters, sparks that soared into the night; but the next was loud and almost at once there was another, and more flying embers and a sudden yellowish flame that leapt quickly to the height of the *San Cristobal*'s foretop, setting fire to her sails and rigging, fire that leapt along her topsail yard and raced upwards in the tarred ratlines on either side, a high background of darting fire to light the swirl and fury of the battle, and Gawdy'd not thought about it or seen it as any cause for hope until suddenly that Spanish trumpet sounded, urgently and high, a note of fear from the direction of the flames, and the Spanish soldiers, still fighting, began to fall back towards their burning ship, shouting one to the other as they retreated slowly behind a barrier of whirling swords. And Grenville roared above the din, *'Saint George! Saint George for England!'* His voice rose high as *Revenge*'s culverins fired again, pulverizing the Spaniard's prow where they must already have penetrated to the powder-room: Grenville shrieked triumphantly, 'Now we have them! *With me, lads!*'

The English pressed forward, madmen, cheering, and the Spaniards divided, broke and ran; their galleon, burning fiercely, already drifted away downwind, her prow destroyed almost to the waterline, her stern rising black behind the mass of flames as she drew off, sinking. Gawdy remembered afterwards the almost animal scream of triumph that he'd heard emerging, incredibly, from his own mouth as, behind Grenville and with Langhorne on his left, he'd sprung forward on the heels of the suddenly demoralized and reeling enemy and cut them down while some begged for mercy and others, throwing away their swords, sprang on to *Revenge*'s bulwarks and thence into the littered, hissing sea where the flames' light was reflected in jagged, leaping flashes and already dozens of men's heads bobbed among the floating wreckage.

He remembered too how the flames which lit the night in an aura of orange, red and yellow hissed into extinction as the *San Cristobal* dipped lower, hard down by the head; how the night darkened as she filled and rolled and sank in full sight of them all, the sea's surface steaming as it swallowed her; all of them were hoarse with cheering as they took cover now against renewed firing from the mountainous galleon still lashed along their larboard side. But it was to the *San Bernabé* that the survivors swam, and Bertendona's men were busy hauling them from the water and launching boats to assist with others; and when the *San Cristobal* had gone completely except for the broken litter of her spars and

134

timbers, rubbish and corpses floating, the night was pitch black again and those marksmen could only fire when flashes from their ordnance showed them targets on the English decks.

Revenge's fire was scant, now, one gun at a time and even that at longer intervals. That men still lived, down there in the gun-decks at the muzzles of the *San Bernabé*'s cannon, was almost past belief: that some still worked the guns, a miracle.

Gawdy remembered Grenville's face peering closely into his, so closely that the jutting beard brushed his nose: he remembered the hands that gripped his shoulders, and the voice, loud and even jocular, 'What, are you hurt, lad? Eh?'

'Nay, sir.' He denied his wounds, and certainly he'd not had time, yet, to give them thought; only Grenville was bloodied like the rest of them, his face marked by a sword-point below one eye and the shoulders of his armour scarred and dented; Gawdy shook his head, and the sheer power of this Grenville's presence filled him with a kind of relief, happiness, so that he felt a smile drawing up the corners of his mouth, and Grenville saw it, and gripped his shoulders harder and roared with laughter.

'By God, Philip, we'll have a tale to tell them, eh? Eh, boy?'

But there was shouting for'ard, then, men yelling and running on the fo'c'sle deck; here, above their heads, they heard the pounding steps of those who'd been cautiously seeking out any English wounded not past aid, now rushing for'ard and down the ladders to the waist. Then all of them were running, a mob again, Grenville at its head and he, Gawdy, somewhere in it, running for no purpose that he knew of except that danger threatened in the bows . . .

San Cristobal had gone – to the bottom, which was at least two hundred fathoms down – and General Don Marcos de Arumburu had been forced to the indignity of swimming for his life among his soldiers, to take ignominious refuge in Don Martin Bertendona's galleon. But now another of the Castillians, the *Ascension* under Don Antonio Manrique, had come up prow to prow, pushing his galleon's forepart into the wedge-shaped gap between *Revenge*'s bow and the *San Bernabé*'s overlapping fo'c'sle. So once again, Spanish soldiers hurled themselves aboard *Revenge*.

Behind Langhorne, Philip Gawdy found himself at first inside the fo'c'sle, a narrow superstructure through which the foremast grew and where the port-side saker now pounded at the new enemy's prow; but outside its for'ard entrance they found the much narrower beak of the ship, the tiny space between the hawse, held securely by three or four men who so filled the space that there was no space for any more, or need of more; they were hard at it, swords swinging, thrusting, and John Creed in the centre of the group shouted over his shoulder in an easy, friendly tone, 'The upper deck, sir, larboard!' Turning quickly back to more pressing business, he caught a driving rapier in his bare left hand and held it aloft like some trophy while his own sword swung powerfully at its Spanish owner's unprotected neck ...

Out again, past that saker as it fired again and flung back, men leaping over it, springing aside, almost caught by its violent and lethal recoil: out to the waist, and up, and here the others who'd been sheltering inside the fo'c'sle when the Spaniard first ploughed in against *Revenge* were fighting now in a line diagonally across the fo'c'sle top: soldiers from the *Ascension* were climbing from their own fo'c'sle over to the *San Bernabé*'s, and from there leaping down to the English deck. But they were hemmed in there, for the deck was small and narrow and the English sailors fought like demons, yelling, thrusting, yielding no inch of deck, knowing that any space surrendered would at once be occupied by Spaniards jumping from the ship alongside. Farther aft, at the waist, they never tried to enter; the bases in that after cubbridge head swept the bulwarks with fast, murderous fire if ever a Spaniard showed himself, and the six-ounce shot was quite enough to pierce an armoured breast-plate.

Grenville pushed forward into the line of fighting men;

their cheering at the sight of him drew answering shouts and challenges from the Spaniards massed on those two over-looking fo'c'sles; but all their shouts were drowned as *Revenge*'s bow guns began to fire. First the culverins in her lower tier, then the sakers above them and the port demi-culverins in the bow-chase; each fired in turn as the unseen gunners down there moved from piece to piece, the flame of each discharge flaring up to light the narrow gap between the ships, faces, flashing armour, whirling swords; most of those swords were Spanish, now, for the English sailors had discarded broken weapons and snatched fresh ones from dead and wounded men on whom they trod and stumbled as they fought.

The guns were silent now, no doubt reloading – if men were there with strength to do it – but there were flames on the *Ascension*'s fo'c'sle. That dream-feeling returned to Gawdy, increasing the confusion in his mind as he realized that he'd seen this before, that it was the *San Cristobal* all over again, that fire growing and spreading aft and brightening and flames shooting up to light the heads of struggling men; the English culverins had bitten deep into her fore peak and powder-room and within minutes all her prow was burning, and Creed and his mates in *Revenge*'s prow had no more use, for the time being, for their swords. They'd dropped them, and were busy pouring water, from the tubs set ready, over *Revenge*'s for'ard timbers to keep the fire from spreading to them.

But as the English cheered and pressed forward towards the *San Bernabé*'s bulwarks as the Spanish pressure slack-ened, a new threat came without warning from the other bow: the fly-boat *La Serena*, flagship of General Don Luis Cuitiño, had slid up alongside the *Ascension*, on her other side; now suddenly the English knew of it when Cuitiño's soldiers, and others who'd boarded her from Manrique's galleon, came swarming over *Revenge*'s starboard bow, taking the defenders on her fo'c'sle in their rear. And al-though the *Ascension* had cast off her grappling ropes and loosed her mizen – to swing herself clear, stern-first, of the vicious bite of a much smaller ship which should in any case by now be past resistance, let alone offence – although that Spaniard was taking himself off as best he could in order to founder alone or anyway out of range of *Revenge*'s guns, the menace of his soldiers was not gone with him. Some he'd put in the *La Serena,* and far more still crowded the *San Bernabé*'s fo'c'sle, still leapt down into any space that opened: and moved forward now as the English wavered, hearing the new assault develop at their backs . . .

Gawdy, who'd been behind that short line of men engaged with the invaders from the *San Bernabé,* by now dazzled and half dazed by the close gun-fire and the brilliance of the flames, turned as the others with him turned, his sword rising by some effort which if it was his own was not a conscious or deliberate one. They'd been inactive, ready to take their places in the line if it retreated and thus expanded, or to step in where an English sailor fell: now within seconds Gawdy and the rest were sword to sword with the Spaniards from Cuitiño's galleon and back to back with Grenville's men, so that the English fought in a 'V' which took up most of the fo'c'sle deck, its wide part aft defending the ladder to the waist, its apex at the shattered, splintered stump of the foremast. As they gained ground or lost it the 'V' swelled and contracted; Gawdy fought blindly, wearily, conscious now of pain from many wounds, fighting for life, not victory, for survival and in hate – yes, *hate*! The deck was slippery with blood; he slid, fell to his knees screaming as a Spaniard lunged down at his head, he saw the wild gleam of wide, dark eyes, an open, red-lipped mouth above a black-haired chin, the mouth open in a yell of triumph as the soldier lunged at this suddenly helpless, off-guard Englishman: it was Daniel Sturgee, the Boatswain, who sprang forward and took the blow on a broken pike-head he gripped in his left hand, returned it with a swift, lightning upswing of his own reddened, chipped and tipless sword that split the Spaniard from beard to crown. Gawdy was up, drenched in Spanish blood: his legs had raised him, not his will: he was up and without conscious thought he'd sprung forward across the soldier's fallen body before that square of deck could be filled by another Spaniard dropping from the fly-boat; he pushed forward, finding Spaniards then on three sides of him, his own sword thrusting at the one he faced, and Sturgee sprang in, joining him as another fell, and that whole side of the 'V' bulged and swung forward, the line intact and driving solidly towards the bulwarks. Amidships the cannon-periers fired, the demi-cannon underneath them – no mistaking that deep boom, that degree of powder-flash – and the sakers, the culverins below *them*, all the guns in the starboard forepart where the *La Serena* had now dragged herself, been hauled by sailors running, shifting grappling-irons aft along *Revenge*'s bulwarks, throwing the last ones when they'd found they couldn't show themselves without attracting the bases' withering fire, throwing, heaving-in, hauling the fly-boat up along *Revenge*'s holed and battered side to give the soldiers a wider platform for their attacks. But Cuitiño had over-reached himself, reckoned too easily on the English guns being out of it by now, reckoned too little on the fact that a Master Gunner such as Josiah Wenman, given half a dozen men alive or a dozen half-alive, would have his guns ready served where they were needed, have linstocks lowering to the touch-holes and the glowing stumps of slow-matches in them, the black serpentine powder spluttering, sparking: the gunners standing aside or dropping against the bulwarks, the thunder and the flame for many of them the last of that, a fanfare to oblivion.

And the end to the *La Serena*, whose Commander had reckoned on too little or too much: listing, filled with dead and taking water in her holds, she drifted out and back, swinging, pivoting with her stern to the English galleon's prow: and the bow-chase in *Revenge* was ready too, the pair of demi-culverins stabbing the presumptuous fly-boat in her beam as she swung around and drifted off to leeward, burning flares to summon help.

Once the guns were loaded, it needed only one man alive to fire them.

* * *

Silence, but for the groans of wounded, the whispers of men who sought their friends and found them: silence even among men who met face to face and gripped hands and because all faces were by now blood-streaked, all men somehow hurt or crippled, knew each other through the masks that battle had left on them: all were freaks, the only strange thing was the silence.

The *San Bernabé* had gone. Not far; Bertendona stood near enough to come aboard and claim his prize, his recompense for Corunna; at a cable's length from the English he succoured Luis Cuitiño's ship. He'd cut his galleon free and let her drift down to leeward of *Revenge*'s smoking, shattered hulk, hoisted his fore-sail and fore-topsail to take him up alongside the *La Serena* and lash that smaller ship to his while the pumps worked at her bilges and he moved her wounded sailors and soldiers into his own already overcrowded decks. For his friend Cuitiño's sake, he tried to keep her floating while pumps and carpenters worked to save her.

But on *Revenge*'s decks, that silence. Afterwards, Gawdy remembered it. He remembered how they'd killed the soldiers who'd remained aboard, and his share of that killing, and the silence afterwards and the dead; and the galleons all around them at a distance, vague dark shapes against the sea and stars. He remembered that the silence was a deep, soft cloak around a kind of victory: that Grenville – who had a musket bullet in the right side of his chest (how long he'd had it, no one knew) and whose face was as pale as milk as he stood swaying in the lamplit Great Cabin, barely hearing Langhorne who was telling him that less than twenty men were left to meet any new attack – he remembered that Grenville had turned to him, smiled crookedly and asked, 'Philip: are you hurt?' and that he, Gawdy, had wondered how to answer when the truth was so plain to anyone with eyes: he remembered the surgeon bending over Grenville, easing him down on a blood-soaked pallet on the deck beside that single, yellowish lamp: Langhorne there and others grouping round, the yellow light and the shadows, slow movements, hollow eyes . . .

The broadside from a fly-boat sweeping past almost at arm's length. The shudder, quiver in the ship. The alarm, the storm of small-arms fire. The burst of Spanish hail-shot that penetrated the Great Cabin's devastated side. Chirurgeon Willoughby clasping his hands like claws across his belly: staggering, his head suddenly thrown back as though tired of the sight of blood he sought the stars above the oaken deck-head, except that his eyes were shut, screwed up: the surgeon falling, collapsing across Grenville's legs.

Grenville struggling, fending Willoughby aside, getting to his feet, shouting to know why *Revenge*'s guns weren't firing, hadn't fired: and Grenville in that moment hit by a metal fragment that opened his head from brow to crown.

The mask of blood as Grenville fell. Men on their knees around him, ignoring Clayborn who at the cabin's farther side had spun round like a top, dropped like a puppet from a broken string. The gasps of horror and concern: a world that floated, swam, a world of nausea and old, dead glories. Wenman, the Master Gunner, stumbling in like some creature out of hell: the croaked report from that bull of a man who'd sunk three Spanish ships almost with his own hands and now led in three other apparitions who with him made up the full tally of survivors from the gun-decks.

He spoke to the lantern, at the soft light that for the moment was enough to blind him: 'All shot's spent, sir.'

Langhorne, on his knees beside Grenville, looked up sharply. John Creed laid a broad, bloodstained hand on Wenman's shoulder. He said in a deep, quiet rumble, 'Hold now, Joss. Sir Richard's hit.'

Beside Langhorne, Pennyfeather looked up and met Wenman's eyes as they began to focus to the light. 'He's not killed, Gunner.' There was a rough sympathy in his tone, a deliberate holding-out of hope, almost as if he spoke to Grenville's brother. Perhaps, in a sense, he did. But Wenman's eyes, bewildered, had moved beyond the Vice-Admiral's prone body and the group around him. Beyond there, on the edge of the circle of lamplight, Wenman saw the body of his son. Chirurgeon Willoughby had done his

141

best with many, failed with most: many had been more dead than living when they'd reached him.

Wenman stood frozen: then stepped forward. Creed moved with him, tightening his hold. 'Joss. Joss, there's ninety others too. Don't blame—'

'Blame?'

The Master Gunner's eyes travelled swiftly round the dimly lamplit cabin. Gawdy met them, and looked away: Wenman probed every face, jerked free of Creed's restraining hand, met Langhorne's gaze as *Revenge*'s Captain rose slowly to his feet, facing the Master Gunner's stare.

'Gunner. The Boatswain's dead. Spaniards killed your boy, not Sturgee.'

(Gawdy remembered then the sight of that sword-hilt in Daniel Sturgee's belly. He remembered that as the Spaniard had turned and made for the bulwarks, dropping the dagger in his other hand and fumbling frantically at the straps that held the armour across his shoulders, he – Gawdy – had cut him down from behind, severing him deeply through the shoulder as the armour dropped.)

Joss Wenman shouldered Creed aside and brushed past Langhorne. Kneeling, he raised his son's body in his arms and cradled it against his bloody, naked chest, and whimpered, gasping, gripping that frail, white body in his massive arms . . .

The others slowly turned their backs, none looking at the others. They watched the hands of the Chirurgeon's Mate as he bound Grenville's head with strips of cloth and bathed his face with water already stained bright red.

Revenge lay sluggish on the gently heaving sea, charred and broken, mastless, waterlogged. Around her at a distance waited the dark shapes of Spanish galleons, motionless and quiet as the night wore on to dawn.

IX

And the night went down, and the sun smiled out far over the
summer sea,
And the Spanish fleet with broken sides lay round us all in a ring;
But they dared not touch us again, for they fear'd that we still
could sting,
So they watch'd what the end would be.

Tennyson
(The *Revenge*: A Ballad of the Fleet)

Daylight revealed, across pale glistening sea below a rising mist, the distant islands' shapes and the closer ring of the Spanish fleet: revealed to those who had stomachs for it the charnel-house of the English galleon's decks.

Daylight illuminated in diagonal spears of early sun the Great Cabin where Grenville lay propped, on his own insistence and against the urgings of the Chirurgeon's Mate, with his back against the truck of the starboard saker. Only his eyes moved, below thick ridges of bandage that criss-crossed and bound his head; he'd not allowed them to remove his sword-belt, and his left hand lay on the hilt of the sword as his eyes moved relentlessly from face to face, probing for reaction, demanding obedience and agreement as he addressed the men who faced him in an irregular half-circle. Some of them had slept; those who'd not woken would never do so now. Eleven men watched his eyes as they roved from face to face. Gawdy was one of them.

'Valiant, resolute men: Englishmen, by God, and shown our foe the quality of that!' The Vice-Admiral paused again, struggling for his breath and, as Langhorne had come to realize from his manner and expressions, against recurrent dizziness or faintness; speech was an effort, a new battle. They waited for the outcome of it.

'Fought such a fight as England, her beloved Majesty, can

143

take pride from: and so do I, as her Commander.' Fighting his personal fight again, the one for breath and consciousness, he looked askew at Langhorne. 'How many live? *Here*, how many?'

'Eleven, sir, and yourself.'

Grenville's eyes closed in something longer than a blink. Then: 'Twelve. Near to ninety prime seamen dead. Men of Devonshire and Cornwall.' Again that pause, the hard rasping of indrawn breath. 'Ninety. We, now – their honour's in our hands. *Their* honour, mine, England's: the honour of this ship.' His voice rose. 'The Spaniards shall not have her, d'you hear? They'll not take a Queen's ship when ninety true Englishmen have died in her defence! Eh?'

His eyes burned at them out of his dead-white face under its bloody turban of tight-bound rags.

'I'll sink her, d'you hear? D'you hear me, damn you? *Sink her!*'

Pennyfeather's head jerked round; he stared at Langhorne in amazement. Langhorne met that stare: looked back at Grenville, and said nothing.

The Master rose slowly to his feet.

'Sir Richard. As ye've said, we've fought our fight, and we've no shame to bear. Ninety dead is ninety dead – and if that's honour, I've enough. Three of their galleons sunk: have they told you, sir, that last one foundered after dawn? I say *enough*, sir; we can seek fair terms and do no harm to our country's honour.'

The fingers of Grenville's left hand twitched at his sword-hilt. His right rose an inch above his thigh, pointing at the Master.

'Captain Langhorne. Arrest—'

'Sir.' Langhorne was standing, too, beside Pennyfeather. 'Sir Richard, with the love for you that all here feel—' a murmur of assent backed it as he paused and glanced at them – 'with that, sir, and not idly said: I must support Master Pennyfeather. If we're to die, sir, we'll do no benefit to England or our naval service. Honour's secure; and if we live, we live to fight again.' His eyes stayed firm, although

144

reluctant, on Grenville's stare of hatred. 'We've fought such a fight, sir, fought against such odds as—'

'*I'll not hear this!*' Grenville spat out the words, his chest heaving violently as he panted in his rage; spots of brilliant red burned below his cheek-bones. 'From you, Martin Langhorne, a captain by Her Majesty's commission—'

'Ay, sir.' Langhorne's voice was quiet. 'Ay, sir. And I'd live to serve Her Majesty more fully. To sink this galleon's not to serve her—'

'By God, Captain, d'you know how many years have passed since a Queen's ship struck her colours to the flag of Spain? Eh? You'd have me play the traitor and do *that*?'

Pennyfeather muttered. 'They'll have no prize, Sir Richard. Never get her to any Spanish harbour. There's holes below the water, timbers strained, the caulking forced. The first strong wind – yea, without that, even! – this galleon's for the bottom. She'll sink without *our* aid.'

Grenville ignored him. He asked Joss Wenman, 'You're with me, Master Gunner? Firm to your duty?'

'Yea, sir.' Wenman's growl held a deep contempt for any who felt otherwise or opposed their own Commander. 'With you sir, ay: and God save you, and damnation to all Spain!'

'Ay.' Grenville had heard, from the Master Gunner, what he expected from them all. He glanced at the two men who stood before him. 'To all Spain: and to traitors, to such mutinous dogs and cowards such as *you*, and *you*!' Langhorne looked down, at the space of stained deck between him and Grenville's feet; but in turning then to Pennyfeather, he found himself staring at the ship's oak side. The Master had gone; Langhorne looked about him, saw only men who wouldn't meet his eyes.

'Which of you are with me, then?' Grenville searched their faces. 'Eh? You, Gunner. Ay, Josiah Wenman. You hail from Bideford, and – why, you served—'

The cabin swung and tilted, and his eyes were blank, seeing nothing but that haze of red shot with yellow morning sunlight, swimming brilliance; then it all steadied and men's forms grew darkly in it and he was looking at John

Creed. He thought, I've been asleep, I dreamt, I never heard their answers. He asked John Creed,

'You – Boatswain's Mate. You're with me, know your duty and allegiance?'

'Ay, sir, I'm with you. And Creed there beside you, Creed the Boatswain's Mate, he's with you. Creed's with you, sir.' But that had been Joss Wenman's voice again, not Creed's; Grenville forced his eyes to focus on the man he'd thought was Creed. It was Wenman. He thought again, I dreamt. Now, where's—

The Master Gunner had stepped closer, and now bent beside Sir Richard, his face working with alarm, lines deepening, matted eyebrows twitching. 'I'm your Gunner, sir. You're tired, sir. Rest, now: won't you rest?'

His low, gruff tones were gentle as if he nursed a woman or a child. 'Be easy, sir—'

Easy – he'd heard it and he thought, Oh, *easy*! That swimming light, the deadness in all his limbs as if he'd been drugged or as if his body slept while his mind, reeling, struggled to remain awake: had they drugged him? So that he'd lie helpless while they struck to Spain? Was Wenman in it too? He lying here while Spaniards came aboard, encroached on English decks without their lives as payment? He, Richard Grenville, lying here while Spanish feet came tramping: was the Gunner in it too?

How many'd answered when he asked, *Which of you are with me?* All? How long ago was it that he'd asked? What had happened since?

Spaniards *here*, possessing, usurping, seizing? What, had the wind risen? That soaring, rising, swaying into blackness! Why'd they not light the lantern, in this dark? Dark – and so warm! The ship burnt, did she? Then they'd fired her? Had Wenman—? He was struggling, trying to shout. He'd not meant *fire*! Oh God, the heat of it!

Didn't they know the Inquisition waited for them if they lived? Why else had he waited to embark those miserable sick? And the galleys: if honour meant so little that it could be twisted to suit a whim for life, what of the galleys?

146

Now rest, sir! Rest!

Rest? What of the feet, the filthy pounding boots, legs like pillars rising in coarse peasant cloth towering, the smell and press and the cries of hatred, triumph, a devil's triumph that, a devil infinitely vulgar, brutal and uncouth: looking up, so high up, such pain up there, a gob of Papist spit hanging in the old man's eye—

Seven, then, and not large for his age. In the year before, 1548, there'd been Papist risings throughout the West; Sir Martin Godfrey had been hanged, others drawn and quartered, and that (they thought) had been an end to that. But now a year later several thousand rebels out of Devonshire and Cornwall, peasants hating the new Prayer Book that used English instead of Latin, had come flocking under Humphrey Arundell and marched on Exeter; they failed there, but Plymouth fell to them, and in Plymouth happened to be the old Sir Richard Grenville, Marshal of Calais, with his wife and a party of gentlemen and ladies; and with him too was his grandson, Richard, then aged seven. They'd taken refuge in Trematon Castle; but by trickery the mob broke in, dishonourable, foul-mouthed, evil-smelling; screaming profanities and threats, cruelly mishandling all inside the castle, even breaking the fingers of the ladies in order to steal their rings. The boy remembered all his life his own childish terror and the shocked helplessness in his grandfather's eyes as he'd looked down at him: the old soldier-poet mortified not just by the indignity and brutality but for the fact that this child should witness it, see him, Sir Richard, impotent and insulted.

In March of the next year, 1550, the old Sir Richard died; suffering still, they said, from the shock and harsh treatment at the hands of that illiterate, Papist mob; and in April, just four weeks later, Lady Grenville followed her husband to the grave.

Forty years ago: but the picture stayed, memory as clear now in the Vice-Admiral's strained and rambling mind as it had been then a harsh reality of childhood: if anything, it was clearer now. The shock was undiminished, he still sweated when he allowed himself to think of it, only the rage

147

and the sorrow had grown harder as the years had passed.

His eyes were open: dull, angry, searching the faces that confronted him in the mixed shadow and sunlight of *Revenge*'s Great Cabin. He seemed unsure, as if the images were blurred.

'Are ye with me, then?'

Gawdy shrunk back into a pool of shadow: it was a question he dreaded facing.

Langhorne slowly, sadly, shook his head. 'Ah – *with you, with you*: yea! In all the fight – ay, and in any other – we're at your command. Yet now, sir, to speak only for myself, since I believe this is a matter for each man's conscience, I choose to live; and – I beg your pardon, sir, your forgiveness.'

Joss Wenman growled, 'By your leave, Captain: the fight's not done, for we've not struck our colours – and shan't do!'

Several agreed with that, moving slowly forward from their corners, muttering assent. One of them was Creed, the Boatswain's Mate, and with him, inseparable as always, the mis-shapen, long-armed Jabez Shaw. Two of the three gunners who'd come up with Wenman out of that butcher's shop of the gun-decks moved over to stand by him, muttering acceptance, blinking tiredly at the sunbeams which lanced in through shot-holes and open ports.

Grenville asked sharply, 'How many then are loyal?'

Langhorne said quickly, '*All*, sir. We're all loyal to you. Only there are some like myself who'd rather live to serve Her Majesty than die to no good purpose—'

Grenville's weakness restrained the burst of rage such opposition would normally have provoked. In a tone that was almost mild, for him, he said, 'England's honour, no good purpose? Ay, Captain Langhorne, I know your voice, though you hide in shadow!'

'Sir, I'm in the sunlight, here in face of you!'

'*Damn* you for your chatter!' Stronger, suddenly! Though obviously his sight was failing. He told Langhorne in a lower but still steely tone, 'Those who disobey me, who'd strike to Spain – that's your purpose? That what your conscience bids you, Captain Langhorne? Traitors and dogs, d'you hear? What, *loyal*, d'you call it? *All loyal?* Lies, and pretence! Lies to dissemble *cowardice*, Captain Langhorne! Master Gunner, how many d'you count with me?'

'Why, sir, there's me and these four others, that's five, and you, sir; by my reckoning, we're six. Your Master's left us, sir, this last hour: so that's six here for you and five against.'

'More men true than traitors then! For that, thank God!' Grenville coughed: drew breath sharply against the pain, paused while it lessened. He muttered angrily, 'The Master's gone, has he? Well, no grief in that . . . Gunner – your shot's all spent – and well, by God! There's powder still?'

'Yea, sir.'

'Good. Then, Master Gunner – accept my thanks, my highest commendation; and – split me the ship! D'you hear me? *Split her!*'

'Aye aye, sir!' Wenman grasped John Creed's elbow, pulling him with him as he moved for'ard, giving Langhorne and the others a wide berth as he passed them. The small man, Shaw, tagged on in Creed's wake like a long-boat towed astern. Grenville called suddenly, surprisingly, 'Hold!'

Wenman stopped, half turned. 'Sir?'

'Those that are with me: is Philip Gawdy one?'

The Master Gunner looked across at Gawdy, inviting him to answer for himself. Gawdy was silent, looked away. Wenman said gruffly, 'Nay, sir.'

'*What?*' Surprise in that, as well as anger! 'What, Philip? You'd die a traitor, then? *You?* My kinsman's nephew?'

'Sir, I—' Gawdy had started forward, upward to his feet, struck his head on the beam above, and he staggered, clutching for support. Grenville's few words had stung him, pierced his soul: he moved towards the Vice-Admiral, drawn to him as if by some magnet, ready now to offer him his loyalty, his life: now, finally, it was a kind of absolution that he sought—

'Hold there, Gunner!'

Pennyfeather, in the cabin's entrance, blocked Wenman's exit. 'Eh, Gunner? Where're you bound, then?'

149

'Upon his duty, Master!' Grenville had recognized that voice, and scowled his loathing of it. 'His duty: and damn you for a traitor! Gunner?'

'Yea, Sir Richard.'

'Do my bidding!'

'Yea, yea.' Wenman turned for'ard again, but Penny-feather stepped squarely in front of him. The Gunner swore, dropped a hand to the sword at his side, a Spanish weapon taken from the deck. The Master never moved: but John Creed's hand clamped like a vice on that threatening arm.

'Nay, Joss. Hear him first, if he brings news.' The big man asked Pennyfeather brusquely: 'Well?'

'I'm come from the Spaniards, lads. From their flagship, that sent a boat to my hail. *San Pablo*'s their name for her; I've parleyed with their Commander, seeking terms.'

'*Traitor!*' Grenville's body writhed and his voice was high.

'*Dog!* By God, you'll hang for this treachery, you'll *hang*! I, Richard Grenville, swear it!'

Pennyfeather seemed unmoved. He said slowly, 'No treachery, sir, to seek honourable terms by which Englishmen who've proved their courage ten times over can return to continue in the service of their Queen.'

Grenville didn't answer. His eyes were closed and the bright colour of his rage had faded; below the rags that wrapped his head, a thin column of blood trickled down beside his ear. Langhorne beckoned urgently to the Chirurgeon's Mate, who'd been sitting with his mouth open, absorbed by the talk around him. Now he shuffled forward on his knees to wring out a piece of cloth over the leather bucket of red water.

Pennyfeather waited until he saw Langhorne turn back to him. Then he said, 'Their Commander's ready to put an end to this. They've enough dead by any reckoning; and three galleons sunk. His own captain killed, too – from *Foresight*'s broadside before our own fight started ... Their admiral's name's Bazan: a shrewd fellow, but honest enough, I'd say – for a Spaniard ... He spoke at length of his admiration for—' the Master's eyes moved to the prone, still body of the Vice-Admiral – 'for Sir Richard Grenville, though they've some other way of saying it, in their lingo. Ay, he marvels at the fight we've made.'

'His terms?' Creed still held the Master Gunner's arm.

'That if we go over into his galleons, he'll allow our lives and freedom. We'll none of us be given to the Inquisitors, nor to the galleys or any other slavery, or ill-used. They'll put us home to England: and—' he glanced at Gawdy, back at Langhorne – 'and the gentlemen may wear their swords.'

Langhorne asked quietly as they gathered round, the separate groups disintegrating, only the Gunner, with Creed and the other man close beside him, still apart, 'He gave you his word for it, this Spanish general?'

Pennyfeather nodded. 'Ay, his word.'

Wenman wrenched himself free of Creed. 'A *Spanish* word, lads! D'you take *that*, rather than Sir Richard Grenville's? Why, *damn* – there's four of us, five, as shan't—'

'Nay, Joss. That's past.' Creed looked unhappy, but decided. 'We've wives, and children to be fed. And – why, *life*, Joss!'

Jabez Shaw dipped his monkey head. 'Life. Ay!' He nodded again, his eyes on Creed. 'Life!'

'We'll sail again, Joss.' One of the gunners had spoken that.

'Fight again!'

'Live!'

'We take our honour with us, back to England!'

'That you do not!' Joss Wenman rounded on them all, on the circle and the chorus of agreement, on the faces smiling at this release from Grenville's own strict code, release from certain death. He told them furiously, 'Mutineers, take honour with you? Your wives want *traitors* in their beds?' His eyes swept over them; then he spat quickly on the boards between his feet. 'By God, I've my Commander's order and I'll—'

Creed and Pennyfeather moved quickly, blocking his way as he turned: Shaw moved up, his long arms crooked and tensed in front of him. The others, too, closed in. Only

151

Langhorne still crouched, watching Grenville, Gawdy at his side now, the Chirurgeon's Mate still busy.

The Master Gunner stood rock-still, staring at the men who faced him. Both of them big: Creed topping him by half a foot: neither of them as badly hurt as he was. He swung round, a cornered bull, glaring at the others crowding in, stopping some of them only with his stare. Those behind him saw the muscles bulge in his back as he turned back to Creed and moved his right arm slowly, deliberately across his own body, the hand of it to the hilt of the sword at his left side.

'You'll prevent me?'

Creed nodded. The Gunner's eyes shifted to Penny-feather. He nodded too.

Wenman said, 'Sir Richard's bound to die: and not one of you fit to serve him! You'd stop me from my duty? *By damn*, then I'll go with him!'

He'd wrenched the sword out as he said it, turned the broken blade of it against his throat, placed left hand over right upon its hilt—

John Creed, and Pennyfeather, sprang forward, grabbing for the Gunner's arms. They'd have been too late if it hadn't been for Jabez Shaw who'd flung himself somehow upwards through those arms, exploding ape-like from the very deck, knocking the sword up so that it gashed the Gunner's chin: then Pennyfeather'd grabbed it, wrenched it out of his hands, and Creed had pinioned him in immense, long arms.

And Gawdy, crouching beside Langhorne, thought, *I haven't moved. I'm with him, but I haven't moved. Now it's over and the cock's crowed twice. Twice, and it's done, and though these others talk of honour all I'll ever know is shame.*

'They'd move you, sir. Carry you into their flagship, the galleon *San Pablo*.'

'*Who*'d move me? Who sends this word?'

'Their general, sir. His name's Alonso de Bazan. He

152

admires you greatly, sir; seeks to give you such comfort as he can offer.'

Those eyelids had flickered; now they opened. The voice came in a whisper:

'*He may do with my body what he list: for I esteem it not.*'

When they lifted him, he fainted.

Epilogue

On Flores, Corvo, Faial, Pico, São Jorge, Graciosa, Terceira and São Miguel, the Azorians still scoured their islands' rocky coastlines for the timber that came up with every tide. In the last weeks the rocks had been piled with it; at first whole ships – fifteen alone flung up on São Miguel – but since then had come almost as thickly the timbers of many others which had foundered or driven against outlying rocks where the sea had battered them in pieces and drowned their crews.

Ricardo del Campo Verde, known to the Protestant English as Sir Richard Grenville, who'd been – for years it had been no secret to the islanders – in league with the Devil, had died two days after the battle in which his galleon *La Venganza* had sunk three Spanish warships (two that same night, the other foundering next morning) and battered others so fiercely that when the storm came up they were easy prey to wind, water and rock. He'd died, that one, in the *San Pablo*, the Spanish flagship, and Don Alonso de Bazan, who strongly loved the Englishman for his valour and reputation and demeanour, had buried him at sea with all the honours due to him. And then at once the wind had risen, risen swiftly, evilly, backing and veering through all the points of the compass, whipping the sea to madness, frenzy, to such wild murderous strength as had never been seen in the Azores in all the memory of man. The Azorians had cowered in their houses, for eight whole days, thinking the storm would swallow up the islands, destroy them utterly: waves rose higher than the cliffs, living fishes struggled in the fields.

The *flota* had arrived from the Spanish Indies: a double convoy, this year's and last's, in all 150 sail. Of that number, only thirty reached Iberian ports. A few, scattered by the storm but surviving it, were captured by the English victual-

154

lers and taken in to Falmouth; the rest perished among or on the islands, overcome in the maelstrom of a sea gone mad.

The English galleon, *La Venganza*, had been the first to founder; she'd taken with her 200 Spaniards out of the *San Bernabé*; Don Martin de Bertendona had claimed her as his prize, and put them aboard as crew.

Sixteen more of Alonso de Bazan's galleons were lost. Ten thousand Spaniards perished. On Terceira alone, 3,000 bodies were flung up.

The wind, now gentle, came from the north-east; and with it on white wings came news from England. Of the safe return of all the English ships to West Country ports: that Sir Walter Ralegh, cousin to Grenville, had proclaimed Lord Thomas Howard coward, and challenged him to a fight with swords. Rumour added that no fight had come about. It added that Her Majesty had heard of it and intervened, forbidden it, commanding Ralegh to future silence, commanding Howard to disregard the insult and the challenge. Rumour could be true: no man, however highly placed ignored Her Majesty's command and kept his head.

But those were far-off things. The islanders needed timber, to rebuild their houses, build new boats. Well, it was there, theirs for the taking.

For three whole weeks after the storm had died they'd done nothing but fish for dead men, but even now as they gathered in the timber, bodies floated in among it.

When they came upon such corpses, they took them up and buried them. Most were battered beyond any kind of recognition, and it was assumed they belonged to the true religion, entitled to its rites. Yet still, as each body was brought up out of the sea and carried across the fields, the islanders came close to peer into its face, crossing themselves beforehand in case this should be the one they feared

155

above all other, the Devil's kin who'd summoned storm and slaughter to avenge his death.

But the one they sought: looked for, yet dreaded finding: that one the sea did not surrender.